BOOKS BY ADAM PFEFFER

Published by iUniverse:

Kolak of the Werebeasts

Twilight of the Gods

The Missing Link

To Change the World and Other Stories

The Day the Dream Came True and Other Poems

The Visitors

The Creation of God

The Amazing Slick McKinley: Greatest Athlete Ever

The Fantastic Flying Man

The Fantastic Flying Man

ADAM PFEFFER

iUniverse, Inc.
New York Bloomington

iUniverse books may be ordered through booksellers or by contacting:

iUniverse
1663 Liberty Drive
Bloomington, IN 47403
www.iuniverse.com
1-800-Authors (1-800-288-4677)

Because of the dynamic nature of the Internet, any Web addresses or links contained in this book may have changed since publication and may no longer be valid. The views expressed in this work are solely those of the author and do not necessarily reflect the views of the publisher, and the publisher hereby disclaims any responsibility for them.

ISBN: 978-1-4502-4689-7 (sc)
ISBN: 978-1-4502-4690-3 (ebook)

Printed in the United States of America

Library of Congress Control Number: 2010912777

iUniverse rev. date: 08/20/2010

The never-ending flight
Of future days.

JOHN MILTON: *Paradise Lost,* 1667

1

The feeling is incredible. Incredible. All you hear is the sound of the wind rushing past you. You may hear the whistle of a nearby bird once in a while, apparently trying to communicate some social message, or the sound of a plane growling in the sky, but mostly you hear the wind. You hear the wind and feel the sunshine, and suddenly, you feel free, truly free.

This is the culmination of all of humankind's dreams. Yes, the ability to fly. Fly like a bird.

I knew nobody would believe it, so I decided a demonstration would be in order. I would demonstrate to the world the absolute power and freedom we were dealing with. I picked New York City, the most populous city in the United States, to display the success of my experiments. This was the hub of the American media outlets and the center of money and power in America. It was a place where anything could happen and usually did. Well, wait until they saw Doctor Tommy Hagenhurst. This would be something they would remember throughout their lives. This was something that would become history. Yes, history.

I felt the wind snapping through my hair, and saw the landscape shifting down below. This is better than any ride I had ever been on. An amusement park roller coaster was truly laughingly juvenile in comparison with this experience. Why, it made driving a car a tedious routine in comparison. This was the essence of freedom, the ability to go wherever one truly wanted. It was the freedom to go anywhere in the world at a moment's notice.

Anyway, I decided New York City would be the place I would go to introduce myself to the world. The media of the world would be alerted, and then I would tell them what I had in mind. It would be the first step to my becoming one of the richest and most powerful men on the planet, a dying planet pleading to be renewed.

Yes, New York was the place to go to be seen by people all over the country. It was the place to go to display new innovations and inventions, the place to stimulate unwavering interest and unlimited financial backing. The Big Apple.

It was about noon when I first soared over Manhattan, being seen for the first time by the lunchtime crowds that swelled into the streets. I steadied my body and stretched my arms out in front of me, trying to make the most impressive pose I could before all of those eager eyes.

Then I saw them -- the reporters, the television cameras, all glaring in my direction. I put my arms to the side and soared to the west. I then waved to all the people down below and headed for the Statue of Liberty. Yes, Lady Liberty herself. I gently landed in her crown and continued waving to anyone who was watching me from below.

It was a grand show, I must say. I waved to the ferry boats, and to both shores, on east and west, and smiled for everyone. Then I jumped back into the air and soared to the New Jersey side of New York Harbor where I would check into a hotel and watch myself and all that had happened on a television.

I knew my life would never be the same again.

2

We have breaking news out of New York. An unknown man was seen soaring above the city skyline today until landing on the crown of the Statue of Liberty. We have reporters in downtown Manhattan and on Liberty Island and video footage of the entire affair. First, let's go to Dean Snow who's standing on Broadway in downtown Manhattan—

Yes, I'm standing here in the theatre district of New York where I witnessed something many people believed was part of some Broadway publicity stunt. But theatre officials assured me what we saw was no publicity stunt, at least not one touting a Broadway play. The man, who remains unknown at this time, was seen flying across the Manhattan sky during the lunch hour in this bustling city wearing only a white t-shirt and tan shorts. (*Video footage of the man flying across the Manhattan sky.*) Why he performed what we assume was a stunt of some kind and where he is at the present time are still mysteries. No one we talked to knew how he actually performed the stunt and what his message actually was. The noontime exhibition made this usually jaded city of millions come to an abrupt halt with many pointing their fingers and shouting to anyone who would listen what was occurring up above. We have some people here who witnessed the demonstration.

"Sir, what did you think of the flying exhibition this afternoon?"

"I think it was some kind of trick, that's all. I mean, I don't know how he did it, but it was pretty cool, anyway."

"And ma'am, did you see it?"

"Why, yes, we were just standing here ready to go to lunch when we saw him up there with his arms stretched out in front of him, just flying in the air. I don't know how he did it, but that man was awesome, simply awesome."

There you have it. Did he do it to make some sort of point, and more importantly, just how did he do it. His flight lasted only a few minutes, but it was clear, this event would linger in the minds of those who witnessed it for some time. Dean Snow reporting in Manhattan. Now let's go to Carol Numar on Liberty Island where the unknown man landed for a short time.

Yes, I'm standing here on Liberty Island in New York Harbor where the unknown flying man landed for a short time before soaring off to New Jersey. Jim Sniff is an official with the National Park Service, who oversees the statue and its island.

"Mr. Sniff, did you see the man land on Liberty's crown?"

"Yep, sure did. We all ran out here shouting to him that sitting on that crown was dangerous."

"And what was his response?"

"He looked at us, smiled, and waved. Then he flew off to New Jersey."

"Did you see any wiring of any kind or anything that was holding him up in the air?"

"Nope, can't say that I did. We were looking for a boat that he might be attached to, but there wasn't one we could see. I don't know how he did it to tell you the truth."

"Thank you, Mr. Sniff."

The man landed on Liberty's crown at about twenty past twelve in the afternoon to the applause of many down below. Many boats on the Harbor slowed down or approached the island, many wondering just how the man was able to accomplish the feat. The only boat seen plowing through the waters of the Harbor, remaining on schedule, was the Staten Island Ferry. We talked to some of the people aboard after they docked in Manhattan.

"Ma'am, did you see the flying man?"

"Sure did. I don't know what he was selling, but he landed right on Lady Liberty and waved to everybody. A real wacko if you ask me."

"Sir, did you see him?"

"Yeah, and the only thing missing was a full moon. When he jumped off the crown, I couldn't believe it. The fruitcake was flying in the sky just like a cuckoo bird."

Whether the flight had some rhyme or reason to it is still open to discussion. What we do know now is that the man flew, that's right, flew, for lack of a better word, to the New Jersey shoreline. Where he eventually landed again, nobody knows. Reporting from Liberty Island, this is Carol Numar—

Well, that's all we have at the present time. To repeat this breaking story, an unknown man, I would say somewhere in his thirties, flew across the Manhattan sky at noon and then landed on the crown of the Statue of Liberty. (*Video footage of the man flying over Manhattan.*) He then flew off to the New Jersey side of New York Harbor. How the feat was accomplished and whether it was attempted for some reason is still not known. But nothing was damaged and it seems evident that it wasn't some sort of terrorist attack, although police are still quick to say the incident is still under investigation.

We will have more details and video footage tonight on the Evening News. Until then, Russell Johnson reporting from New York. We now return you to your regularly scheduled programming.

3

It is clear this is just another example of an event occurring in the Terrorist Age. It was definitely something engineered by the Techie Generation, who believe they are capable of achieving anything that has anything to do with a technological solution. Flying is just another technological problem that can be solved through science.

Yes, that's very interesting, Doctor Lune. So then you believe it is possible for human beings to fly—

I don't see why not. If it has some sort of implications for improving conflict on this planet, human beings will find a solution. You must remember that war and a belief in some sort of God holds the centuries together. They are the very elements of human history.

Yes, and do you think that will ever change?

I think it must for human society to advance. But things might get worse before they get better. I and a lot of my colleagues see a new age of Zealots in the near future who will shout about God and war until they are finally vanquished many years from now. Once we lose that primeval need for God and war, the world will progress and eventually become a technological and medical paradise.

Yes, that's very interesting. Why do you think someone tried a stunt such as flying without any assistance at this time?

Well, you see, I think many people believe there is nothing new or original anymore and that everything has been done and the planet is old and dying. I see this as an attempt to do something original, innovative, in a world where most people believe they have seen everything and done just about everything.

Yes, and do you think there was a trick to the whole thing?

There might have been, but I caution you that the Techie Generation believes everything is possible, everything has a technological or scientific solution. The trick may have been discovering a solution to the problem of flying by oneself, not the actual flying.

Thank you, Doctor Alvis Lune for your expert insight. We will be back after these commercial messages—

I just flew all night from Chicago and, boy, are my arms tired. (*Laughter and applause*) But I want to tell you, ladies and gentlemen—

Feel the freedom of the skies on National Airlines—

We're Jet Flying doo doo doo doo.
We're Jet Flying—

SPECIAL REPORT

We interrupt your regularly scheduled programming for this special report.

Yes, Russell Johnson here in the newsroom. The so-called Flying Man was seen over the skies of Manhattan once again. He was seen flying over the west side of midtown Manhattan just a few minutes ago and is making his way to the east side of the city.

(*Footage of the Flying Man in the skies over Manhattan*)

There you see him making his way to midtown Manhattan. He is flying above the tallest skyscrapers in the area and seems to be smiling. There, now he looks like he's turning towards the lower east side of the city. He now looks as if he is flying towards City Hall. (*The Flying Man is seen with his arms outstretched flying over the city*) We have a reporter at City Hall, Dave Squiff. Dave?

Yes, Russ, I'm standing out here on the steps of City Hall watching as the so-called Flying Man comes toward us. We are hoping he might land and make a statement of some kind or else tell us what he plans next.

(*Cameras are following the Flying Man as he glides across the Manhattan sky*)

Yes, now, I do believe he's coming this way. We'll stay with you until we know for sure.

(The Flying Man soars over City Hall and then dives down and makes a smooth landing on his bare feet in front of reporter Dave Squiff)

Hello there, sir, I'm Dave Squiff, may we have a few moments to talk to you?

Hello, Dave, it's nice to meet you, I'm Doctor Tommy Hagenhurst.

What kind of doctor are you?

Well, I'm actually a scientist who works for Mediworks in south Florida.

And you can fly without any kind of assistance?

That's right, Dave, I have found the secret to flying like a bird without any need of assistance of any kind.

How is that possible, doctor?

I think I better explain that at another time. Right now, I better be off—

Halt right there! Police!

Is this man under arrest, officer?

Yes, that's right.

On what charge?

That's all for right now.

As you can see, there's a whole platoon of police officers here who have their guns drawn and are arresting Doctor Hagenhurst—

(Police are seen on the steps of City Hall holding guns and surrounding Doctor Hagenhurst and the television reporter)

Doctor, doctor, do you have something to say to anyone watching?

I'll have to talk to you at another time.

Sir, you're under arrest. Please put your hands behind you—

(Police are seen taking Doctor Hagenhurst away in handcuffs)

There you have it. Police have arrested Doctor Tommy Hagenhurst for his quite astounding flights over Manhattan without any kind of mechanical assistance. Doctor Hagenhurst, a scientist who works for a company called Mediworks in Florida, has apparently discovered some way for a human being to fly. What that secret is we will surely learn in the days ahead. Reporting from the steps of City Hall in New York, Dave Squiff—

Quite extraordinary. Russ Johnson back here in the newsroom. We still don't know on what charges the police will book Doc Hagenhurst. But we will have that and much more on tonight's Evening News. Until then, Russell Johnson reporting. We now take you back to your regularly scheduled programming.

This has been a special report. We now return you to your regularly scheduled programming already in progress--

4.

Let us through. Book this guy on charges of disturbing the peace, disorderly conduct and obstruction of justice. Take his picture and then lock him up.

Okay, step over here, sir. Don't move for a moment. There, that's good. Okay, step over to the sergeant.

Name?

Doctor Tommy Hagenhurst.

Age?

36.

Height?

6 feet.

Weight?

190.

All right, put him in a cage.

Doctor? Someone has posted bail for you. You're free to go. I just want to caution you that there are reporters outside the police station and if you want to go out the back way, we'll show you where it is.

No, that's all right, officer. I'll deal with the reporters.

Okay, doctor, then you are free on bail.

Thank you very much.

Doctor, doctor, do you have some kind of super powers?

No, I don't.

But you can fly, isn't that right?

Yes, that's right.

When are you going to reveal the secret, doctor?

At the appropriate time.

Is this just some stunt to make as much money as you can, doc?

No, I think there is a benefit to flying. If that means getting money for such a discovery then I think I am well worth it.

What's the gag?

There is no gag, gentlemen and ladies. I have discovered the secret to flying.

Are you going to use it to help the planet, doc?

Yes, of course.

You're going to defeat evil and save the planet?

I told you I don't have any super powers. That's all just comic book stuff. But what I have is real. As real as breathing and walking down a tree-lined street.

Is your laboratory down in Florida?

Yes, that's correct. It's easier to fly down there, you know.

What's the matter, doc, you can't fly in the winter?

It is rather more difficult.

Is that why you're wearing the skimpy clothing?

You have to be as light as possible to fly.

Do you have a wife and kids, doc?

Not at the present time.

You going to fly over Manhattan again?

I might.

Are you prepared to be arrested again?

If it's necessary to make my point.

And what is that point, doc?

That many things are now possible for human beings, such as flying, and in order for progress to occur, one must embrace the scientific community.

Like giving you lots of bucks, doc?

It might if people want these new discoveries to be used for their advantage.

Where you staying the night, doctor?

No comment. Thank you very much everyone.

You can't believe it, Dexter. I'm here in front of the police station where that Flying Man was taken. He just came out of the station to talk to all the reporters. Man, you should have seen all those lights. Bright as summer out here. Yeah, that's right. Then, you won't believe it, the guy walks away from the reporters and soars into the sky. That's right, he was flying.

What? I don't know how he did it. He won't tell anyone until they give him Fort Knox.

Yeah, yeah. He wasn't bad looking, kind of cute. I'll send you a picture. I took it while he was talking.

No, I'm not going to sleep with him. I have you, honey.

A beer? Sure, sugar, there's a convenience store just down the block. I'll call you back when I'm inside the store. Okay, honey, bye.

This is the Evening News with Russell Johnson.

The so-called Flying Man, a Doctor Tommy Hagenhurst of Florida, was arrested and booked in midtown Manhattan today after making two flights over New York City claiming he has found the secret to unaided flight.

Hagenhurst, who is 36, told reporters he had no super powers and would reveal his secret for flight at the quote, "appropriate time."

The scientist is employed by Mediworks in south Florida. When reached for comment, the firm said they had "no comment."

Police said Hagenhurst was arrested on charges of disturbing the peace, disorderly conduct, and obstruction of justice. He was released after Mediworks paid his bail, and after talking with reporters, flew back into the dark Manhattan sky—

Yeah, Deenie, he flew right past my window. No big. He looked like some kind of dork or something. Wonder what the hell he's been smoking. He thinks he's some kind of freakin' bird or something. He was practically naked. Yeah, he's a bird all right. Flapping his arms like some geek, don't you know. Geez, what's his mama thinkin' anyway--

5

DOC FOR THE BIRDS

By Ellis Burke

Doc Bird landed back on his feet.

The Florida scientist, known as the Flying Man and Doc Bird, was released from police custody yesterday after flying unaided through the skies of Manhattan.

His real name is Doctor Tommy Hagenhurst, 36 years old, and has his own laboratory at Mediworks in south Florida. And Doc Bird insists he hasn't any super powers. That's right, he's as mortal as you and me.

"I'm not a comic book character," he said yesterday standing on the steps of a midtown Manhattan police precinct. "I'm real, and I'm not from some foreign world sent here to save everybody."

But Doc Bird can fly, and that's no joke.

"Yes, I discovered the secret of flying without any aid or assistance," he calmly told reporters. "But I can't reveal that secret at the present time."

Doc Bird said he won't reveal the secret until he gets lots of cash. You see, his amazing scientific discovery comes at a price. He ain't exactly Superman.

He explained he made the two flights over Manhattan as a demonstration of his flying powers. Those flights took him to the crown of the Statue of Liberty and the steps of City Hall. He was then surrounded by members of the New York City police department and taken away.

After spending about an hour in police custody, Doc Bird was released. He then talked to reporters and said he wasn't angry about being arrested.

"They were just doing their jobs," he said. "I was just doing what I had to do."

He was asked if anybody can fly. "If they know the secret," he replied without any details. "That's all I'm going to say at the present time."

He said he planned on staying in New York and would sleep at a local hotel. Even the Flying Doc Bird has to get his rest, you know.

"Well, I'll see all of you again some time," he said, walking away from the lights and the reporters.

And then Doc Bird quickly ascended into the sky and flew away into the darkness. Everybody agreed after watching the display that his secret was well worth the money.

-END-

DOC BIRD FLIES OVER MANHATTAN

Click to watch the video.

That's right, I'm able to fly. There is no trick to it it's a product of scientific know-how. I can't reveal the secret at the present time, but I assure everyone this is not some comic book stunt. This is real.

Doctor, doctor, do you have some kind of super powers?

No, I am a normal American just like you. I'm sorry to say I am not the product of some child's comic book, but a real person. Thank you very much everyone.

Doctor, doctor?

Wow, do you see that? He's flying away into the sky! Holy cow!

End of video

6

They wanted me to be God or Santa Claus, giving out things for free. That was the human race, all right. They prized material possessions above all else, considered those with a lot of money intelligent and successful, but when it came to answering their prayers or saving their very lives they expected it to be free of charge. God, Santa Claus, Superman and the Justice League of America did things out of the kindness of their hearts. They expected no payment in exchange. Unbelievable.

I sat around thinking about it and decided I really had no choice. There were a lot of poor, sick people out there and I would be the only one to really have the power to do something for them. Me. Doctor Tommy Hagenhurst. I mean, I couldn't even make the high school football team. Now they wanted to know if I was Superman.

Well, I was no Superman, but I was the only one on this dying planet who could actually fly. So I decided I would help them, just temporarily, you understand, just long enough for them to realize that what I had discovered was worth all the money I was asking. In time, they would see what I had was invaluable. At least, that was what I was counting on.

I decided I couldn't afford to wear some sort of costume. It would more than likely just weigh me down. To fly, one had to be as light as possible. The most advisable thing to do would be to go naked, but I knew I couldn't do that. So I put on a pair of tight shorts and a t-shirt and I was on my way.

The first person I saved in New York was a woman who was about to be hit by a speeding taxi cab. I swooped down just at the last minute and grabbed her by the collar of her blouse. The blouse ripped and she let out a scream that could be heard miles away, and then I lifted her into the air and carried her to the sidewalk. I let her down gently and she accused me of sexual harassment and wanted me to pay for her damaged clothing. Gee, thanks would have been quite enough, ma'am. She never offered to even tip me. All I did was save her life.

The next person was a kid falling out the window. He must have been about six years old, but I told you I was no Superman. After falling out the window on the sixth floor, I caught him in my arms. But without super powers, this seemingly easy exercise is not so easy. He weighed more than I anticipated and we both began falling to the concrete below.

Well, I decided there was no way I was going to let the kid fall out of my arms, so I twisted and twisted until finally he ended up falling on top of me. We hit the ground pretty hard, with him on top of me. The kid was quite all right, but I was pretty bruised. Did anybody care? Nope. They picked the kid up in their arms and carried him away hooting and hollering and leaving me on the concrete to fend for myself. No thank you. They assumed because I could fly, I was naturally forced to save them. They thought I had no choice in the matter.

Well, I limped away and decided I would only continue this nonsense for a few more days. I first wanted to see what the media made of the whole thing. Maybe after a few headlines and video shots things would change. I mean, they had to. Right?

Before going home for the evening, I noticed a man holding a gun on the upper west side. He was running out of a small grocery store with a huge bag in his hand. Now remember, I told you I was not Superman. I had no super powers, and that meant if a bullet hit me, I was doomed. So I stayed high up in the sky, and then I noticed a big rock on top of the roof below. I swooped down took a hold of the rock and threw it down at the man's head. I'm glad I used to play a lot of baseball in high school because that rock hit him right on top of the skull. He collapsed to the sidewalk, lost his gun, and was captured by some big guys down below. This time, I didn't wait for a thank you and flew off into the growing sunset.

I was pretty tired as I flew to my hotel room in midtown Manhattan. You think saving people is easy? Well, it's not, let me tell you. I was bruised and tired and all I wanted was a bath, a glass of wine, and some clean clothes. Then I would sit down in front of the television and see what they really thought of me.

I began to realize being a hero was not what I really thought it would be. I really wonder why Santa Claus never demanded payment of any kind. And why God answered all those various prayers for just a thank you and a simple amen.

7

This is the Evening News with Russell Johnson.

The fantastic Flying Man, also known as Doc Bird, began saving people today on the streets of New York City.

But, according to the people saved, the brand new hero is definitely not as graceful as Superman or Batman. Here's Robert Croller with our report.

He might not be as strong as Superman or as inventive as Batman, but Doc Bird got the job done.

"He tore my blouse." (*Video of Pamela Nussberger*) "He seemed very awkward and not prepared to save people."

Ms. Nussberger was one of the first people to be saved by New York's new hero. That's hero, not superhero.

And while he may be a rather clumsy hero, most people agree he's a bona fide hero nonetheless.

"He caught me when I fell from the window."

That's six-year-old Felix Rodrigo, who fell from his six-story window until Doc Bird plucked him from the air. Apparently, however, the boy was heavier than the new hero thought, and they both tumbled to the cement with the boy landing on top of the fantastic Flying Man.

"He saved him." (*Video of a smiling Maria Rodrigo, the boy's mother*) "I hope Doc Bird is all right."

One more save like that, and somebody just might get hurt.

"He's definitely not Superman. The kid was too heavy for him. I've never heard of a weak superhero."

But Eddie Manago may be wrong. Each hero always has his own set of powers. Doc Bird's powers seem to be flying and well, good luck.

"He hit that crook right on the head. He has very good aim."

You see? According to Damian Harris, America's newest hero has perfect aim as well.

The armed thief was taken away by the police after being knocked unconscious by a rock dropped by Doc Bird right on his head. Let's see Batman do that.

And what do the police have to say?

"We never asked for his help and ask him to stop attempting rescues without any qualifications."

The police spokeswoman seemed to indicate they won't be flashing a signal into the sky in the near future.

"I hope he continues saving people. This city needs him."

And Laura Softley is one of many New Yorkers who feel that way. So here's to Doc Bird, maybe a little clumsy but someone who is real. A hero New York City is embracing until, well, until Superman appears. Right now, Doc Bird is the only one who is not just a character in some child's comic book. Reporting from midtown Manhattan, Robert Croller--

8

DOC BIRD SAVING 6-YEAR-OLD FELIX RODRIGO

Click to view

Ahhh, my baby!

Oh my God!

What the hell is that?

Swwwooosh!

He's saving the baby!

That guy is flying, man!

Wooooo, look at him!

He's got him!

No, he's gonna drop him!

Look out!

Shit, he grabbed him!

Is the boy all right?

They hit the cement, oh no!

No, he's got him all right!

That crazy flying dude did it!

Wild, man!

What a bomb!

END of video

DOC BIRD SOARS

By Richard Tippler

Look up in the sky – it's a bullet, it's a plane…it's only Doc Bird.

Yes, Doc Bird, who isn't Superman. But so what, he's the best thing this city has.

Yes, Doc Bird, able to leap tall buildings in a single bound. And then fall to the cement clinging to the one being saved as he rolls on top of him. Oh, well, nobody's perfect.

This guy is the working stiff's hero – a real average in-your-face hero who does nothing easily. Yes, Doc Bird's our man all right.

He saved Pamela Nussberger and only tore her blouse in the process. Not bad.

She would have been hit by a speeding taxi cab. Not with Doc Bird soaring through the air.

Then there's the kid, Felix Rodrigo. Caught him falling out a window and hung on to him as they hit the concrete with the kid on top. Nobody's perfect.

But the real kicker occurred when the Doc plunks down a rock on a gun-wielding man's head. That's a perfect game, no doubt.

Not everyone's in love with this city's newest hero – the police say he should stop saving people and obey the law. For now, Doc Bird is the law. And that's a comfort to a great deal of people in this city, perfect or not.

END

9

We're talking here to Doc Bird, the fantastic flying man, who saved two people and then dropped a rock on a gunman preventing a robbery.

Okay, how can you fly?

I really can't reveal that secret at the present time.

But you can fly!

Yes, I can fly.

You know what they say about men who can fly—

It's all true. Yes.

So are you just going to save everyone?

I hope so.

But what do you get out of it? I mean, these people don't pay you—

No, but just helping people is thanks enough.

He's a real stud, ladies and gentlemen. I mean it.

Well, thanks, Jessica. I'm only doing my best.

Your best is better than most, I can tell you that—

Well, thanks.

Is there a special person in your life? Tell, tell—

Not right now, but I'm working on it.

Ladies, did you hear that? What turns you on, Superman?

A lady who knows what she wants.

Hey, hey, ladies, what do you say?

(Applause)

Is he a stud or what?

(Applause)

Those shorts are getting tighter—

(Applause)

Oh, come on, Jessica.

Doc Bird, ladies and gentlemen, the newest hero in New York, who soars above the skyline and saves those in need. We'll be back after this—

After a busy day of saving people and preventing crime, I kick back with an ice-cold Brewsky. Yep, that's right, as good today as when it was first brewed by Judah Brewsky in 1881.

There's nothing as good as a Brewsky after a full day of saving the human race. And I don't worry about getting filled up because Brewsky has the refreshing clear taste of a light beer. It's as good flying high over the city as it is kicking back at the end of a hard day.

Hi, Superman.

Believe me, nobody's perfect, but a Brewsky is as good as it gets.

Brewsky.

Fluffy shaving cream has just made saving the world a whole lot easier.

Just ask Doctor Tommy Hagenhurst, the fantastic flying man. He starts every morning with the white, fluffy foam of Fluffy shaving cream.

It feels great and smells fantastic. Just like me.

So even if you're not Superman, why not start the day like one with Fluffy shaving cream?

I know I do.

Who knows? The next person you save might be yourself.

Hey, babe.

Fluffy shaving cream. For those looking to get close.

Take it from me, Doc Bird, Fluffy is the hero of shaving creams.

Fluffy.

When I'm not flying above the city, I'm driving through it with my Toyota Rocket. The Rocket is the ultimate in comfort and safety at an affordable price.

Whether you're driving through the city or the green countryside, the Rocket will make your trip a pleasant one with fuel to spare. Electric or gas, the Rocket will take you where you need to go.

(Someone flying through the air and landing on top of the car.)

Can't fly? Then why not save yourself and others with a luxurious ride in a Rocket.

All the world's heroes are driving them these days.

The Rocket.

10

I was becoming a star. Yes, that's right, a celebrity in an age of celebrities. They expected me to know everything and to provide wisdom to their dreary everyday lives. A star for everyone to look up to and talk about. And the money that came along with it wasn't too bad, either.

It didn't matter to me that most people in this age of stardom and superstardom were actually off their rockers. The crazed adulation was something that came along with all the money. They wanted to hear or see something that would light up their lives, make their senseless existence more hopeful and enjoyable, and maybe inspire them to similar greatness. Yes, everyone wanted to be a celebrity. It was the goal of most of the masses. Some tried to sing, some tried to dance, as if singing and dancing were really that important in this world of ours. But no matter. Whatever would grab the attention of the audience was fair game to these aspiring fools.

I was no different. I wanted to sparkle on the stage just like all the rest. What we were supposed to provide was another question, but that didn't matter. People wanted to laugh, cry, smile, and applaud. It made no difference that most of it was momentary and very forgettable. We were stars, damn it. Stars.

Because I could fly, I was asked to appear on most of the talk shows. I didn't mind, it was great publicity. And that publicity led to commercials and all kinds of bonuses. Hell, I was thinking about writing a book already.

Doc Bird, the Fantastic Flying Man. That was me. And I planned to use that stardom to do everything I always dreamed of. Sex, cars, and peace on earth. That was what I was shooting for.

The trick, of course, was staying on top for longer than fifteen minutes. I had it all planned out. I would be a star of stars. The oracle of interviews. Yes, that was what I had planned for the world.

11

Let's bring out that hero of New York, Doc Bird—
(Applause)
Hello there, doctor—
Well, hello, Nege. How are you?
Well, the question should be, how are you?
Fine, just fine.
You okay after saving those people? We heard you had a rough time—
(Laughter and applause)
No, I'm fine, fine. You'll be reading about it very soon.
That's right, the doctor is going to come out with a book about his experiences, isn't that right?
Yes, that's right, Nege.
That's just great! (Applause) *Are you still going to save people?*
Well, I'm going to take a little break, but I'm not retiring the shorts and t-shirt. Not yet. (Applause).
That's just great, doctor. Now I hear you want to do a little song for the upcoming holidays. Isn't that right?
That's right, Nege. It's called, "Christmas Snow."
Great. Here's Doc Bird then with his holiday song, Christmas Snow—
Christmas Snow is falling
Down upon the ground,
And I am calling
From this Christmas snow-town.

Christmas snow is falling,
There beyond my door,
And peace is calling,

From the ruins of war.

Christmastime is back again,
Christmastime is here, my friend.
Christmas snow is all you see,
Oh-oh, it's nice to be
Spending Christmas with you…

Fantastic. Doc Bird everyone—
We'll be back after this--

12

This is the Z, ZLP, playing this town's newest holiday hit, "Christmas Snow," by the flying Doctor Bird. The song is already number one on the Billboard charts and is so hot, it's going to melt all that snow coming down. Like Santa doesn't have enough problems...

Doc Bird – Christmas Snow – Official Music Video (HD)
This is the new video of Doc Bird's Christmas Snow.
Click to view
23,803,094 hits

Well, I bought my first guitar when I was 10. Or maybe my mother bought it for me. I'm really not sure anymore. Anyway, I played the songs popular at the time.

And now, this song, "Christmas Snow," is a number one hit. How about that, ladies and gentlemen?

(Applause)

Why do you think people like it so much?

Well, I like to think it captures the holiday spirit. A song that talks about peace and spending Christmas with one's loved ones. I think that's the kind of song people want to listen to.

Great, doc. And now I hear you have another song for us, although this one has nothing to do with the holidays.

No, but it does have something to do with love and human beings. It's called, "Sky Bound."

Here's Doc Bird doing "Sky Bound."

There upon a velvet ride,

The wind is zipping by my side,
I'm sky bound.

Then I look into the breeze,
It gives a wink so silently,
I go round.

Clouds moving to my left and right,
Stars are still sleeping from the night,
And I go—
Sky bound.

Doc Bird, everyone, the Fantastic Flying Man—
Peace is half a fist, everybody. Thank you.

13

DOC BIRD SOARING

By Dave Finch

Hot.

That's what Doctor Tommy Hagenhurst is right now. Hot.

He's the hottest thing to come down the pike in a long time. That's what they're saying among Hollywood's elite.

He hit the scene with his flying exhibition over New York, and then astonished everybody by saving people from sure calamity. Oh, that Doc Bird.

Now he's got the number one song in America, "Christmas Snow," and another sure hit on the way. This bird can rock and that's no lie.

So what's next for the Bird?

How about a book and his own TV show? Yeah, that's right, this bird is soaring high.

If that's not enough, his phrase on television, "Peace is Half a Fist," is now the hottest thing on tees all across the nation. People all over the world are using the peace sign from a fist more than they did in days gone by. All because of the Bird.

"I thought it up in my dressing room," says the Bird. "Between the massage and the onion dip."

That's our Bird, all right.

And now we hear the Bird is hanging out with the beautiful Tao Dade, whose new movie, "Loving Mr. Big," is a smash hit at the box office. Some year for those two.

So how about it Bird?

"We're just friends," he told us. "But things might be heating up pretty soon."

That's our man, Doc Bird. Boy, is he hot in every way.

DOC BIRD AND TAO DADE TYING THE KNOT

By Dave Finch

Yup, it's official.

Doc Bird, the Fantastic Flying Man, and actress Tao Dade are tying the knot.

They only met only a few weeks ago. But Doctor Tommy Hagenhurst, who is at home in the skies saving New Yorkers from certain disaster, says the two hit it off right away.

"We were made for each other," said the doc. "She's me in drag."

The two plan to get married in February somewhere in the South Pacific. In the meantime, Doc Bird is building a love nest in California.

"We'll be close to the television and movie studios," he told us. "You'll be hearing a lot more from us in the coming days."

And with that, he flew off down the street with his new beloved.

-END-

14

I was well on my way to having it all. I mean, the women adored me and the house and car were bigger and better than anything I could have imagined. I was a star all right. Bigger than anything that had come down the pike in a long time. They didn't know who they were dealing with. I could do more than just fly. And that was a pretty good talent in itself.

I knew I was lucky. Not many had the good fortune or talent to make it to the top. This was in a society that had tired of the white male and now favored women or blacks or African-Americans or Hispanics or Native Americans or whatever. Everyone was going to get their shot. Yeah, right, except anyone who had money or didn't have the right connections. But, you see, I did something that made them say, yes. I flew through the air. How can anyone possibly say, no, to that feat?

There was so much crap people were selling, and I was no exception. I guess it was all how you looked at it. To some, it was crap, to others, revelation. It was all a matter of opinion. That was the fame game, the art game, or practically any other game in town. It was all based on someone's opinion. Whether you liked something or hated it, it was all a matter of personal taste. You could give a reason and an explanation for liking something or hating it. Anyone could do it. It was called, criticism. And anyone could be criticized or complimented for seemingly the exact same thing. It was all how you presented it and what you said. The greatest works of art in human history rested on a shelf of bullshit. Bullshit made the world go 'round, and I could bullshit as well as anyone.

Anyway, I was now a star. I had money and was reasonably good-looking, and therefore, had women falling over me wherever I went. It was a good life, except now I was getting married. Tao was beautiful and was reasonably intelligent. I mean, she could remember her lines from a script.

How intelligent did a woman have to be, anyway? As long as she was willing to perform sex in an adequate manner, everything was cool. Right?

Anyway, I decided I would be happy with Tao. I knew I couldn't resist some of the women I would meet on the way, but Tao seemed open to sexual experiences and that was fine with me. Some of the women I met were outrageously gorgeous, maybe even more beautiful than Tao. And they wanted me. Nay, not wanted me, craved me. Yes, I had hit the big time. Big time. And there was no turning back.

15

Hello, ladies and gentlemen, we're here at the wedding of Doctor Tommy Hagenhurst, the Flying Man, and Tao Dade, the gorgeous Hollywood actress. The couple have just arrived here in Hollywood, will tie the knot, and then be off to somewhere in the South Pacific. Man, what a wedding it will be! Now we send you to Jova Mackey—

Hello, everyone, and welcome to Beverly Hills! In just a moment, you will see the bride and the groom make their way into the church. We will stay here until they disappear inside. The wedding itself will be off limits to the media. And now, here comes Doc Bird, Doctor Tommy Hagenhurst, the Fantastic Flying Man, in a black tux. Very handsome, don't you think? He's making his way to the church, and what a crowd there is. Oh no, Doc Bird is rising into the air. Yes, I think he's going to fly above the crowd before he makes it inside the church. Unbelievable.

There he is, Doc Bird, flying over the wedding crowd here in this posh area of Beverly Hills. I wonder if he's going to save someone. Now he's landing in front of the church entrance, waving to everybody, and then goes inside. What a great show for everyone! Now he comes back out and puts two fingers in the air. No doubt, he's telling everyone his famous phrase, 'Peace is half a fist.' Really unbelievable for everybody.

And now, here's the bride, the beautiful Tao Dade, making her way through the crowd dressed in white. How lovely she looks, don't you think? She makes her way through the crowd, throwing what looks to be daisies to the crowd gathered around the church. What a spectacle!

Everyone who's anyone in Hollywood is here, of course. And they'll be treated to a memorable affair of the highest quality, you can be sure of that. Well, there's Tao waving to everyone and then she steps into the church. Superb!

We can't show you the actual wedding, but we did want to show you the happy couple arriving at the church for today's nuptials. Now back to you, Bill—

What if something happens on your way to saving someone?

Are you protected?

Well, Doc Bird, the Flying Man, is. He's covered by the friendly people at Good Life. Good Life is the insurance you keep so you don't have to worry about things going wrong.

And doesn't that make life a little less complex?

"Good Life is a good friend."

Yes, and Doc Bird knows if anything happens on his way to saving the world, Good Life will be there to help him.

Good Life, a good friend.

Doc Bird, the Fantastic Flying Man, was probably the first groom in the history of the world to actually fly at his own wedding. That's right, while some grooms are head over heels in love with their bride, Doctor Tommy Hagenhurst actually took it to the skies.

"It was just Doc Bird's way of saying that he was in love."

And that wasn't the only guest impressed with the Flying Man's demonstration of love.

"He must really be in love," said another.

This all happened as the wedding party was making their way inside the church. Doc Bird was being overcome by a large crowd of people when he decided it was much safer a few feet above.

(*Video of Doc Bird flying through the air toward the church*)

And, yes, he made it to the church on time.

(*Video of the doctor landing and going into the church*)

And what did his bride, the gorgeous Tao Dade, think of the stunt?

"That's why I love him," she said.

The actress told us she thinks the world of Doc Bird and he can fly anytime he wants to. The flighty couple made it official inside the church and then were off to a South Pacific island. No word if the couple plans on taking a plane to the destination or if Ms. Dade will fly on Doc Bird's back.

A story that's really for the birds, don't you think? Tom Reynolds reporting--

16

Live from Hollywood, this is the Doc Bird Show—
Today's guests are Artie Howard and Liz Crockett—
And now, America's Number One Flying Man, Doc Bird—

Hi, everybody, and welcome to today's show. You know on the way here I stopped off at the Natural History Museum and marveled at all the dinosaurs. There was a brontosaurus, a Ty Rex, and even a pterodactyl. Those things were huge flying reptiles. I mean, they must have been fifty times the size of a bird. And then coming back from the museum I walked past the statues with pigeon poo all over them and I began to wonder that if those pterodactyls were fifty times the size of a bird and there were a great many of them in those days, just what the heck did cavemen's statues look like? And you think history is a bunch of shit?

Thank you, thank you.

Here's something I was thinking about: if there are no gays in heaven, what do God and the angels do about their hair?

Thank you very much. We have a great show for you today. Artie Howard and Liz Crockett are here and I'm about to take off—

Wheee, here I go soaring through the air—

I'll come down after you watch these next messages. Wooooo, all right—

I may be able to fly without any help, but you're going to need someone to get you where you're going. To get there the right way, use Air Wings.

Air Wings has the most comfortable seats and we don't hassle you about extra bags. There's plenty of room on a Air Wings jet, and you'll even get a sandwich on most flights.

Hey, even I can't fly by myself all the time. That's when I use Air Wings, comfort in the sky.

Air Wings, comfort in the sky.

Tell them, Doc Bird sent you, and have a good flight.

Hi, everybody, we're back and I'm going to sing you a little song. I hope you enjoy it——

One thing you should know,
If you want to go
Flying
Yes, I'm flying
Flying
Yes, I'm flying

A bird is overhead
And over my bed,
I'm flying
Yes, I'm flying
Flying
Well, yes, I'm flying

In the breeze
Oh, I'm flying
Well, yes, I'm flying
Flying
Yes, I'm flying
One thing you should do,
You know it's up to you,
Flying
Oh, yes, I'm flying
Flying
Well, yes, I'm flying…

(Applause)

Thank you very much, ladies and gentlemen. We have a great show for you. And we'll be back after this--

17

This just in to the newsroom—

Doc Bird, the fantastic Flying Man, was seen flying over the city with a woman in his arms. According to eyewitnesses, the woman was not his wife, Tao Dade, but another actress who some identified as Gina Vulva. Vulva is, of course, the sexy actress who has starred in a number of films, many of a very sexual nature. Some say the pair were wearing very little clothing and were shouting and groaning in the air.

And, yes, now we have confirmed that the woman in Doc Bird's arms was, indeed, Gina Vulva. There was no immediate comment from either Doc Bird or his wife, Tao Dade. We will be closely watching this story and will update you if the information becomes available—

DOC BIRD'S MILE HIGH CLUB

By Lee Pile

Who was that spotted in the air with Doc Bird over Hollywood the other night? None other than Gina Vulva, that's who.

And according to our sources, the two were making whoopee high over Glitz City, unconcerned with those far below.

"They were going at it pretty good," said one eyewitness. "It was definitely rated NC-17."

The doc, Doctor Tommy Hagenhurst, is, of course, married to sexy Tao Dade. So what made him stray? Our sources say Doc Bird met Vulva at a Hollywood party and was immediately impressed with her. The sultry star of many sex-oriented films was mutually attracted to the fantastic Flying Man.

Our sources say that to impress Vulva, the doc offered to fly her home leaving his gorgeous wife behind.

The doctor then apparently informed Vulva that to fly one had to be as light as possible, and the two of them stripped down to their underwear. No word if the two were drunk at the time, but the police are now searching for them to hear their side of the story.

And a juicy, sexy story it is, according to our sources.

"They were mutually attracted to each other and went flying," one source explained. "It was a new twist on the same old Hollywood love affair story, that's all."

Our sources say Tao Dade left the party in a huff and vowed to bring that "flying clown" down to earth. We'll see about that in the coming days.

In the meantime, Doc Bird and Gina Vulva are the newest members of the Mile High Club.

The only thing left to see is if Doc Bird is forced to eat crow.

-END-

Click to watch video

Okay, baby, let's go flying.

Awesome, doc.

Holy shit, they're up there.

They're doing it.

They're up there doing it.

Holy crap, look at them going at it.

That's Doc Bird up there.

Look at them go, man.

Man, what a show.

There they go, man.

What a show.

Yeah, great.

END

TAO: What the hell were you doing, doc?

DOC: We were just hanging out.

TAO: They tell me you were fucking her in the air.

DOC: I was just showing her how I fly, Tao, honey.

TAO: Don't give me that Tao, honey, crap.

DOC: But nothing happened, Tao, honey.

TAO: That's not what I heard.

DOC: It's all bullshit. That's the only thing they know how to report.

TAO: Oh, bullshit, doc, they only report what they see or hear.

DOC: Nothing happened, Tao, honey.

TAO: Do you mean it?

DOC: Of course.

TAO: Then I have nothing to worry about?

DOC: Nothing, Tao, babe. I was just showing her how I fly.

TAO: All right, doc.

DOC: All right, babe. You know you're the only one for me.

TAO: I hope so, doc.

DOC: Give me a kiss and let's get to bed.

TAO: I can dig it, doc, honey.

DOC: Yes, let's dig it, babe.

18

I was in deep shit. This whole fame thing was getting to me. I had the need to want it all, and it seemed as if everyone was willing to give it to me. There was a catch, of course. It was either the women or the money that got one into trouble, and with me, it was the women. I just couldn't control that thing in my pants. No, sir. It wanted every beautiful woman I looked at. And with my fame increasing, I usually got what I wanted.

Now Tao was beautiful, there was no doubt of that. And under normal circumstances, we probably could have been happy. But these were not ordinary conditions. No, sir. Every beautiful babe in Hollywood wanted to go to bed with me. And my thing thought that was just how it was supposed to be. I, on the other hand, had my doubts. It was one thing looking and talking to these beautiful bodies, but once you got involved sexually, it was over. It was then they thought they owned a piece of you or something. Once you did it with a woman, there was no going back. They would haunt you for the rest of your life.

You take Gina Vulva. She was pretty hot and made my thing jump just looking at her. She was all hot for me, too, and then after we did it, she was all over me like I belonged to her now or something. Well, I didn't want to belong to her and I didn't want her belonging to me. I didn't know what to do and I was afraid that would be the end of my marriage to Tao. So I tried to end it, but Gina wasn't having it. No, not without a substantial financial penalty of some kind. I didn't know how to get rid of Gina. And I didn't know if I wanted to be stuck with Tao for the rest of my life.

I thought about it and decided I needed time to sort the whole thing out. In the meantime, I would add more meaningful songs to my repertoire and hope that would sustain my image until everything was revealed. The public wouldn't care as much about my personal life if I was giving them quality work to think about. That was my strategy, anyway.

So I sat down and worked at my songwriting and everything else, and hoped that would be enough to ride out the coming storm.

19

Live from Hollywood, this is the Doc Bird Show—
Today's guests are David Castle and Lady Vavoom—
And now, America's Number One Flying Man, Doc Bird—

Hi, everybody, and welcome to today's show. You know a Roman Catholic priest has said that gay people don't get into heaven. I was thinking about that and then I thought who decorates all the clouds for the different holidays up there? I mean, who makes all the costumes for the different parties up there? No gays in heaven? I mean, doesn't that leave John Wayne to make the fruit punch or something?

Thank you, thank you.

Yes, and I was thinking what happens if a barking dog begins to stutter? What the heck would that sound like?

Thank you very much. We have a great show for you today. David Castle and Lady Vavoom are here and I have a very important song to sing to you after these messages—

I need all the energy I can get, so before I go off flying, I drink Flash energy drink.

Flash gives you the needed energy to take care of all those things you need to take care of. So maybe it won't help you to fly, but Flash sure can give you the energy to put your world in order.

That's why I drink it all the time. So take it from Doc Bird, Flash is the energy drink that helps you get it done.

Flash energy drink.

Hi, everybody, we're back and now I'm going to sing that important song I promised you. I hope you enjoy it. It's called, Hungry Man—

O Hungry Man
His sunken eyes gaze across a land
Strangled by a blight

And Hungry Man
The twilight pours across his hands
Vanquished by the night.

O Hungry Man.

Giving out a hand
To every hungry man
There throughout the land
To every hungry man.

O Hungry Man
His body caught within a storm
Ravished by his doom

And Hungry Man
Torn apart by the forlorn
Cries that stain the moon

O Hungry Man

Giving out a hand
To every hungry man
There throughout the land
To every hungry man.

O Hungry Man…

(Applause)
Thank you very much, ladies and gentlemen. We have a great show for you if you stick around. We'll be right back after these messages—

20

This just in to the newsroom—

Another woman has stepped forward to say she was involved in an affair with Doc Bird, the fantastic Flying Man. This is the second woman, in addition to Gina Vulva, who has said she has had an affair with Doctor Tommy Hagenhurst. No comment from the doctor or from his wife, the actress Tao Dade. We'll pass on further details to you as they become available. Until then, we return you to your regularly scheduled programming—

Lara Toris says she had an affair with Doc Bird, and is now telling everyone so that he doesn't hurt anyone else—

Lara, how long did you have an affair with Doc Bird?

For two and a half years.

Did he take you flying at all?

Yes, we went flying every so often. Tommy was good to me when we were alone, you understand. I didn't know he was married for a long time.

He hid that from you?

No, not really. I don't think it ever came up.

Why are you stepping forward now?

I think what Tommy is doing is terrible. And I think there are more girls involved. He was always telling me he loved me and I believed him. Then when we were in bed, I saw him texting to another woman. This was right after we made love.

What do you think about Doc Bird now?

I think Tommy has a problem. It's just like a drinking problem or a drug problem or something like that. Tommy has a sex problem, and that really isn't a joke. He can sleep with anyone he wants, and he often does. At least, that's what I've seen.

Are you trying to warn other women?

In a way, yes. You see Tommy and me had something special. At least, that's the way I felt. He was always telling me how special I was to him and that he loved me and everything. And I believed him. This is what I want other women to know.

One woman says that Doc Bird may have been playing around with as many as 35 women behind his wife's back—

That's right, Roberta Melons, who stepped forward today as the newest woman who had an affair with Doctor Tommy Hagenhurst, the fantastic Flying Man, says that she is far from being the only one to sleep with the flying hunkster behind his wife's back. His wife, of course, is the gorgeous Hollywood actress Tao Dade.

While Ms. Melons is the third woman to publicly admit to having an affair with the flying doctor, she says she knows the doc was playing around with at least 35 women.

"I would say, yes, at least 35 women. That's a conservative estimate."

Roberta Melons made the bombshell announcement at a press conference in Los Angeles.

Doc Bird or Tao Dade were unavailable for comment, but neighbors say there has been a lot of activity at the Hagenhurst Beverly Hills mansion in the past few days.

Ms. Melons told reporters that, like all the women who have stepped forward, she made love to Doc Bird at various sites and he told her he loved her very much and would get a divorce from his wife.

"He used to tell me I was an example of truth in advertising. My last name told everyone exactly what made me special."

Ms. Melons said she was going public with the information, so that the flying Doc Bird can do something about his obvious sexual addiction. Nobody, however, has seen Doc Bird since the revelations have come out. Bob Simpson, World News, Hollywood—

This just in—

Doc Bird has lost all of his endorsements. The announcement was made in the wake of the revelation that the fantastic Flying Man was having an affair with at least 35 women behind his wife's back. His wife is the gorgeous Hollywood actress Tao Dade.

With the affairs revealed by a spurned girlfriend, Doc Bird now stands to lose millions in the lost endorsements. The Flying Man endorsed everything from energy drinks to luxury automobiles. One advertiser who is not pulling out is Trojan rubbers.

Many are now waiting for the flying man to make an apology to everyone in light of the affairs. In the meantime, girls are coming out from various walks of life to tell their story of their affair with Doc Bird. Some say the number could go as high as 50.

It is still not known what his wife's reaction to the whole affair scandal has been. There is still no word as to the status of their short marriage. We will have more details on this breaking story as they become available—

DOC STUD

By Carl Rote

Holy harem, Doc Bird is a stud.

King Solomon nothing, this fantastic Flying Man was soaring over the city with babes in his arms. They say the number is close to 65. No lie!

"He told all of them he was in love with them," says one close associate. "He really knew how to handle a harem."

And a harem it was! A harem in modern America.

And what about his wife, the beautiful Tao Dade, you ask? Close friends say she was gone after number three stepped forward. You go tell her there were just a few more. Like 62 more!

"I think she's staying with friends," says one close associate. "Taking a lot of showers."

This is the most miraculous story in many years, with many marveling that a man could satisfy, and keep secret, 65 gorgeous women. And many of them are stepping forward to tell their side of the story. Insiders say there might be as many as 40 books being published about Doc Bird's exploits. Most of them, they say, are sure to become bestsellers.

"Sex sells," says one publisher. "Is there any other reason that we know about Casanova and Don Juan?"

The biggest book of all, Doc Bird's memoirs, are also scheduled to be published sometime this year. And what about something from Tao Dade? The possibilities are endless.

"You'll be reading about Doc Bird's affairs until Christmas," says one insider. "There are a lot of people involved."

Meanwhile, all of the endorsement deals have ended. The only one left is Trojan rubbers. Nothing more to say.

There's still no word from Doc Bird himself. No explanation, no apology. Just a new nickname: Doc Stud.

END

21

We're talking here with Tasla Butts, who says she is one of the many women who had a fling with Doc Bird—

Tasla has just written a book about her experiences with the fantastic Flying Man entitled, "Eight Miles High." She is here with us this morning to talk about some of the more controversial portions of her book—

Now you did some wild things with Doc Bird, didn't you?

Oh yeah, Jennifer, Doc Bird was absolutely crazy about the way he had sex. One time he told me to lie on the ground with my legs spread apart. I watched with amazement as he flew into the sky and then came floating down with no pants on.

He did it with you flying down from the sky?

Oh, yeah, we had all kinds of crazy lovemaking episodes. He took me flying many times in which we would take off all our clothes and then make love while flying over cities and towns.

Was this a joke to Doc Bird?

No, Tommy was very serious about his lovemaking. He was willing to do it almost anywhere and anytime. I think he thought of it as a great thrill in his life and he didn't take it lightly.

What was the wildest place you made love?

Well, Tommy took me to the top of the Washington Monument one time, Jennifer. We made love with everyone going about their business down below. He loved having sex at various American landmarks. One time it was the top of the Capitol and one time the top of the Lincoln Memorial.

How about the White House?

We never made it there, although Tommy told me he did it there once with somebody else. You see it was very hard to get clearance to fly up there, and Tommy was reluctant to ask.

But he was allowed to do it there one time?

That's what he told me. I don't know if he was telling the truth or not, but I imagine if the president gave the okay, Tommy would definitely have no problem with doing it there.

Very interesting. This is all in your book?

Yes, and there's a lot more. Tommy was very willing to experiment where he made love, and since he could fly, he made love at all sorts of places. He was like a huge bird with a huge urge to make love wherever he wanted. I must say it was quite enjoyable being with Tommy.

Do you intend to see him again?

Oh, no, I guess it's all over now. But I'll miss Tommy, I really will. He was a sweet guy who was very talented.

Do you have anything to say to him?

I would just tell Tommy that it's time for him to admit he had a problem. I think it's time he apologized to everyone.

Thank you, Tasla Butts, whose new book is out today. We'll be right back after this—

LOVE ON TOP OF THE WHITE HOUSE

By Billie Hart

Well, at least, Doc Bird was very patriotic. We might call him "Doc Eagle" after a former girlfriend said she made love to the fantastic Flying Man on top of the White House with the permission of the Secret Service.

"The president must have known," said Marie Cosita, who described herself as Doc Bird's Latin lover. "No one said anything about it."

Ms. Cosita, who was one of the Flying Man's reported 73 lovers, said she flew to the top of the White House in Doc Bird's arms and then proceeded to make love to him without any objection from below.

"No one tried to stop us at any time," she said. "It was like it was one big joke."

No word from the president about this alleged affair, although a spokesperson told reporters the incident was "under investigation." There was also no comment from Doc Bird, who seems to be hiding somewhere on the West Coast, and his wife, Tao Dade.

Ms. Cosita says the White House wasn't the only landmark where the couple made love. The two apparently made love on top of the Capitol and Mount Rushmore.

"We did it right on Washington's head," she told reporters. "It was a thrilling experience, just thrilling."

Park officials said the couple had no permission to do anything on Washington's head. "It's a case of trespassing on an American landmark," explained one official. "The two of them should be arrested."

There is, however, no real proof that the couple ever visited the historic landmark. "Maybe somebody will come forward with some video evidence," said one official. "Then we'll know for sure."

The new revelations have only added to the growing list of women who say they have had an affair with Doc Bird, Doctor Tommy Hagenhurst.

Some believe the count will go as high as 100.

"He was a flying sex maniac," said one official. "We hope we catch him one of these days while soiling some American landmark."

-END-

We're talking to Jolesa Mone about Doc Bird—

We did it on the Sphinx one time. Tommy flew me there and then he suggested we do it right on its head.

Were there other sites?

We did it on the Eiffel Tower one time and then he took me to the Great Wall of China. That was a lot of fun.

Are you still in love with Doc Bird?

I don't know if I'm in love with Tommy, but we did have quite a lot of fun doing it all over the world.

Did you know he was married?

He might have mentioned it one time. Tommy and I had something special and nothing could ruin that. Not even a marriage he cared little about.

Did he tell you there would be a divorce?

Tommy told me there was little love between him and his wife. He said she was a cold, selfish bitch who didn't care about anyone. She liked the money Tommy was bringing home, however. He knew that about her.

He said she didn't care about him at all, but really enjoyed spending his money.

Did you go flying with Tommy on a regular basis?

No, not really. But he did take me to the Holy Land where we made love on the Wailing Wall, the Dome of the Rock, and the Church of the Nativity. Tommy said it was his way of bringing about world peace. Tommy was funny that way.

Talking to Jolesa Mone—

We are following this breaking story—

We're here in Los Angeles where Doctor Tommy Hagenhurst has called a press conference. We don't know what he'll be talking about, but we hope he sheds some light on all the affairs he has been reported to have engaged in—

Here's Doc Bird—

Thank you all for coming here today. I know you have heard all the reports of my many love affairs and I think it's time I apologized to the public for anything that might have been said or done in the past. I say, the past, because anything you might have heard I did is quite over. I regret any pain it might have caused anyone and insist that many stories you have heard are either exaggerations or not true at all. I apologize to anyone and everyone and promise you will see and hear a more responsible and mature Doctor Tommy Hagenhurst in the future. Flying is a noble act and shouldn't be abused by anyone. This is something everyone will have to be prepared to decide when I finally reveal the secret to the world. Until that time, I will try to do my best to make this a safer planet. Thank you.

There you have it, Doctor Tommy Hagenhurst apologizing to the world and then flying off into the Southern California sky—

What do you think he meant by saying he was going to try to make this a safer planet?

Suki?

Well, I'm not sure, but he could mean he might start saving people again.

That's exactly what he meant, Suki. He's going to try to clean up his act and take to the air—

Thank you, Jimmy.

Do you think people will forgive him?

I think he sounded sincere and we'll just have to see what he does in the future.

I think they'll forgive him, but they won't forget.

Thank you everyone for your incisive comments. We'll be back tonight with the news of the world. Until then, stay with this network to bring you the latest in the Doc Bird sex story as it develops. And now we return you to your regularly scheduled programming--

22

Live from Hollywood, this is the Doc Bird Show—
Today's guests are Julie Wow and Timothy Grant—
And now, America's Number One Flying Man, Doc Bird—
Hi everybody and welcome to today's show. We're going to start off today's show with a song. I hope you like it—

And on and on
The call for peace
That sometime soon
The guns will cease

And then you know
The time will come
We'll see some love
From everyone.
Peace, oh, peace
In the world.

So join us now
In our prayer for peace
For the time
When the guns will cease

And in our hearts
There's a better world
To share between
Every boy and girl

Peace, oh, peace
In the world

Can't you feel the peace?
Peace of mind
Can't you feel the peace?
Throughout all time

And on and on
The call for peace
That sometime soon
The guns will cease

Peace, oh, peace
In the world…

Thank you, thank you.

We have a great show for you today. Julie Wow and Timothy Grant are here on our last scheduled show. So sit back and enjoy and we'll be right back. But, first, I'm going to go flying—

We'll be right back—

Hi, everybody, we're back. I'm no longer doing the commercials, but I did have a little song to share—

Peace and war
And suffering round
Time to lend a hand

Love and hate
And heavenly bound
Through the winds of sand

Every man
Every man
Every man understand

Every man
Every man
Every man needs a hand.

Light and dark
And traveling round
Doing what you can

Sky and ground
A harmony found
Swirling through the land

Every man
Every man
Every man understand
Every man
Every man
Every man needs a hand...

(Applause)

Thank you very much, ladies and gentlemen. We have a great show for you. And we'll be back after this—

Welcome back to the Opal Show. We have with us today Hubba Johnson, Tai Chen, Lynndie Mendez and Cammy Nipolo, all of whom have had affairs with that fantastic Flying Man, the eminent Doctor Bird—

So, evidently, the doctor liked diversity in his women. It is said he did a whole United Nations worth of women behind his wife's back. We're talking every racial group one can think of in the world. In the world, ladies, yes, that's right. And he took them places. Oh, didn't he now—

Hubba—

HUBBA: Oh, Tommy took me wherever I wanted to go. That was what was so sweet about Tommy. I mean we made love in the Statue of Liberty torch and on top of the United Nations.

On top of the United Nations. He just flew you up there and pow, he made love to y'all.

HUBBA: Pow is right, Opal.

What about you, Tai?

TAI: Tommy was good to me, Opal. He really was. We made love on top of the Taj Mahal—

The Taj Mahal, ladies. What do you think about that?

(Applause)

Where did he take you, Lynndie?

LYNNDIE: We made love on the Great Pyramid at Giza and Big Ben.

Big Ben? Is that right? I hope it didn't start ringing at the wrong time, y'all. This guy really knew how to show a girl a good time. What do you think, y'all? What about you, Cammy?

CAMMY: Tommy and me had what I call, a religious experience.

Oh-oh, where did he take you, Cammy?

CAMMY: We did it on top of the Vatican—

No, you can't be serious. Didn't the Pope get upset or something?

CAMMY: No one stopped us, Opal. We did it on the Vatican and then on the roof of the Sistine Chapel. It was so great.

I imagine it must have been. You did it right on top of Michelangelo's Creation, how appropriate. So the doctor was somewhat religious, is that it, Cammy?

CAMMY: No not really, Opal. You see we also did it on top of the Kremlin in Russia.

Ouch, so the doctor really didn't favor anyone over anyone else.

CAMMY: That's right, Opal. We had a great time.

It must have been freezing—

CAMMY: No, not really. We flew there on a late spring day. Tommy said it was the best time to make love there.

Okay, I guess he should know. Wow, how hot is that, y'all? To make love on the Vatican and the Kremlin. This Doc Bird was one sexy guy, wouldn't you say, y'all? Well, is that all, ladies?

HUBBA: Well, Tommy took me to Rio one night and we made love until morning below the Jesus statue. That was pretty good, y'all. Tommy was one slick cowboy, let me tell you.

Oh, I hear you on that, for sure. Was the doctor a good lover? Hubba?

HUBBA: He was pretty good, Opal. I mean he really knew how to take care of a lady.

TAI: He was very coordinated, Opal. This man knew how to fly and we understood that after spending some time with him.

LYNNDIE: Yes, a very good lover, Opal. Tommy was a doctor. I mean he knew the human body pretty well.

CAMMY: Like I told you, it was a religious experience.

Well, thank you, all of you, for being with us today. We'll talk more about ol' Doc Bird in a moment. We're coming right back—

DOC BIRD AND TAO DADE CALL IT QUITS

Doc Bird will be flying into the sunset and Tao Dade is free to keep loving Mr. Big. That's what we hear from sunny California. The fantastic Flying Man left the Beverly Hills mansion the two had shared and was last seen flying south. No word from Tao Dade, whose movie *Loving Mr. Big* was a big hit at the box office. Some say Doc Bird had as many as 120 lovers while married to Dade.

Click to view the video

\This is the Evening News with Russell Johnson.

Doctor Tommy Hagenhurst, the so-called Flying Man, reportedly left his wife, actress Tao Dade, after she filed for divorce. Doctor Hagenhurst, who also is known as Doc Bird, is said to have had at least 120 lovers while married to Dade, who starred in the movie *Loving Mr. Big*. For more, we go to Kelly Nelson in Beverly Hills, California—

All is quiet at this sprawling Beverly Hills mansion tonight as the occupants have reportedly left the premises. Doctor Tommy Hagenhurst, better known as Doc Bird, was seen leaving the house earlier today and then flew off toward Mexico. Tao Dade, his beautiful wife, was reported to have left soon after. She drove off in a car, her destination unknown.

There have been reports of the two fighting for days over the reports of as many as 120 women having an affair with the flying Doc Bird. Many of the women are still coming forward, many describing romantic flights to exotic locations around the world.

Doc Bird has already issued an apology for his indiscretions and has vowed to make up for his reckless behavior.

Ms. Dade has vowed to collect half of everything in Doc Bird's possession, according to court papers filed in Los Angeles.

Thus far, Doc Bird has lost most of his advertising endorsements and his TV show. It is not known what effect the apology will have in his future public endeavors.

One thing seems certain: Doc Bird will end his many affairs with a variety of women from various racial backgrounds. The affairs took him everywhere from Mount Rushmore and George Washington's head to the Kremlin in Russia.

The world may never be the same.

Reporting from Beverly Hills, this is Kelly Nelson, Evening News—

This is Doc Bird—

I made a few mistakes of my own so I'm urging all of you to engage in safe sex and take along Trojan rubbers.

A rubber is the safest way to have sex and Trojan is the preferred brand of most.

Trojans make sex safe and pleasurable and does no harm to your wallet as well.

So take along Trojans and rest easily.

Trojan rubbers. The brand Doc Bird uses.

23

It was over. Not just my marriage to Tao, but my life as a media superstar. I had had enough, anyway.

It was really all about ego. All these stars thinking they were so great, and in the end, leaving behind very little to get excited about. That to me was the defining feature of the twentieth century: ego. Everyone blowing their horns about their own names and producing very little to remember them by. Most of it was self-indulgent crap. This was the greatest generation? Yeah, right, all because they defeated Hitler, an egotistical madman, in a war that was righteous and necessary. It was righteous and necessary because the biggest egomaniacs of all time were ruling countries. You know all their names: Hitler, Mussolini, Stalin, Churchill, Roosevelt, Hirohito, etc. It was a century of ego. Everyone screaming their names at everyone else with very few having the right to say anything at all. Most wrote books about the righteous and necessary war and became stars.

Well, I had become a star and I had found it somewhat unfulfilling. Yes, I guess the sex was good, but it also became overemphasized. The truth of the matter is it all became, including the sex, so rote, so repetitive. Some of the girls were sweet, but in the end, there was very little to remember them by. There was nothing that they said or did that was so extraordinary or memorable. They were all affairs of lust, rather than of heart or mind. Even Tao left nothing that I would remember in years to come.

I had had enough. So I ended up packing my things and moving to a small apartment in Westwood, California, right next to UCLA. I wanted to think about the possibilities of the future and didn't want to be disturbed. All I knew was that everything was over. Over. I had to think of something new to do that would give me some form of enjoyment and fulfillment. That thing was, of course, flying.

I was still the only one on this dying planet who could fly without any assistance of any kind. I would use that gift, that talent, that product of science, to improve the world in some way. It was the only thing I would really enjoy doing for a while. I thought about it and then decided to try it out for a while. See what the possibilities would be. I would try to change my life and the world at the same time.

24

This just in to the newsroom—

Doc Bird, the fantastic Flying Man, is apparently in the saving business once again. According to police, he interrupted a robbery when he swooped down from the sky and dropped two wooden baseball bats on the alleged thieves. They were knocked to the pavement, and the police subsequently retrieved the weapons. We will have more on this breaking story tonight on the Evening News—

DOC BIRD KNOCKS TWO OUT OF THE GAME

Doc Bird is back on our side, everybody! Yes, that's right
He has returned to saving people from the perils of our age.
Vote in our poll on how you feel about the new Doc Bird—

He threw two big wooden bats down on the crooks' heads. He was better than Babe Ruth.

That's Paula Hall, who was one of those watching the robbery in Santa Monica unfold, when the fantastic Flying Man himself, Doctor Tommy Hagenhurst, showed up.

He sure knocked those two screwballs out of the park—

(*Video footage of Doc Bird hitting the crooks with baseball bats*)

That video was shot in Santa Monica by one alert eyewitness. And that might mean Doc Bird has left media stardom and has gone back to saving people. We'll ask Pokey Birnbaum—

Well, I certainly think it means Doc Bird is once again thinking about helping the public. And he might just be getting the hang of flying without any assistance.

Thanks, Pokey—

The incident happened at about 2 in the afternoon when two gunmen entered a Santa Monica store and demanded everyone hand over their money and goods. Doc Bird was apparently flying overhead just as the gunmen emerged from the store. He quickly retrieved two wooden baseball bats and proceeded to drop them on the gun-toting men. The men were subsequently knocked to the ground and their guns recovered after they slid across the pavement. No one was injured in the incident and all the money and goods taken were recovered.

He was superb. A real hero. I don't believe all those stories with the girls. This is the Doc Bird I know and love.

I don't think Pisa Griffith is alone in her praise of Doc Bird today. We will have more details as they become available—

25

So I was back to saving people. This time, however, I knew a little bit about how it was done. This time I wouldn't jeopardize my body or my health by trying to do anything that called for super powers of any kind. I would use my brain to figure out how to prevent tragedies from occurring.

The first thing I thought of was heavy objects. By just dropping these objects on potential thieves, the crime would be prevented. It worked the first time I tried it with the wooden baseball bats. Those things were heavy. They were heavier than I realized, and before I dropped them on the crooks, I almost fell to the pavement. Oh well, I was determined to learn the right way to do it before I was finished.

The next thing I thought of doing was just defecating or peeing on them like a real bird. Because I wore only shorts and a t-shirt to fly, it was rather easy to expose myself and let them have it. The first person I tried it on was a man trying to steal somebody's handbag. He was running down the street and I couldn't find anything large enough to drop on him. So before he got away or became lost in the crowd, I let him have it with an extraordinarily large bowel movement. I hit him right on the top of the head, and he immediately staggered, gagged, and fell to the pavement. The stench was unbelievable, but the man was captured and the handbag recovered. Hey, you've got to do anything you can to make something come out right.

The next time a man was running away from the police after robbing a store and I let him have it with urine. It was the only thing I could think of at the time to prevent the crime. He kept running even as I drenched him with everything I had. Then he slipped to the pavement, rolled over, and began choking before the police caught up with him.

I knew some people would call these tactics out of bounds or something, but I didn't think so. I was determined to do anything I could to stop the criminal from carrying out his nefarious plans. If that meant using any of my bodily functions to help prevent the crime, then that is what I resolved to do. The main thing was stopping the crime from happening.

26

DOC DOO

By Morgan Keller

Who says crime prevention is a bunch of shit?

Well, maybe, only Doc Doo, I mean Doc Bird.

That's right, Doc Bird did his namesake proud by dropping a bundle on an escaping crook. And that bundle didn't happen to smell like roses if you get my drift.

"If that was the only way he could stop him, then that's fine with me," said one eyewitness, a George Lerner.

The police are not so forgiving. "I think it was a disgusting example of vigilante justice," complained a police spokesperson. "He has no authority to carry on these crime prevention exhibitions."

But that's not what the people think. "I think he's doing his part to stop crime in the world," said Lee Farrell. "Whatever he uses is fine with me."

No one seems concerned that this is the same Doc Bird who was accused of having affairs with more than a hundred women while married to the beautiful actress Tao Dade.

"None of those romances have been proven," said Roe Hudd. "If this is the way he wants to apologize to everyone, then that's what he should do."

Meanwhile, the crime rate in Southern California is steadily declining. "He really shouldn't be getting in the way," said one officer, "but he is helping the department catch some of these criminals."

What about using feces to catch these criminals?

"You won't get me to say he's doing a great job," said one officer. "His methods are questionable, but the results are good. I think the guy's all right, but don't quote me on that."

So the only ones making a stink these days are the crooks, and that's the way everyone in Southern California likes it.

-END-

We're talking to Doc Bird, the flying hero who has begun saving people again—
What about your mother and father, are they still alive?

My mother was a white nurse and my father was a black doctor. They both died, but not before encouraging me to help people through the miracle of science. You see I became a scientist and then discovered this secret to flying.

So then your parents couldn't fly?

No, but they did steer me in the right direction.

And are you going to tell all of us how to fly, doctor?

Not at the present time. I don't feel the human race is ready to fly at this time. There are so many things we have to take care of before we would be ready to go off flying.

What are some of those things we must do, doctor?

Well, I think we first must be at peace throughout the world. I'm not happy that man insists on carrying out wars. These wars are always justified, although I don't believe the justifications any longer. They always tend to bring up World War II as a just and necessary war. Well, that might have been true, but the wars that occurred after that world war were all justified in the same way. I just don't see many of those wars as achieving anything of real value, and I think the excuses for the wars were based on paranoia and domination.

So then why did you decide to begin saving people once again?

I think the best thing I can do with my discovery in science is to help people and the planet in some way. I can't be at all places all the time, but I can use this scientific discovery to make the planet a better place to live. I think, in time, I will decide to reveal the secret of unaided flight and then everyone on the planet will be able to participate in protecting the planet.

So you are going to continue to save people?

Right now, yes, for the time being. I might not have any real super powers, but I do know ways to help stop crimes and assist the people of this planet.

More with Doc Bird after these messages—

Doc Bird was spotted back in the Big Apple yesterday, rescuing people from a burning building.

"He saved about ten of us who were trapped," said Lasha Brown. "He kept making trips up and down until everybody was out."

Although the fire department frowns on civilians helping to save people, one fire official said Doc Bird was a blessing to those ten people trapped in the building.

"No one else could have done it," he said. "If it wasn't for Doc Bird, those people would likely have perished."

This is the same Doc Bird who only recently left his wife, Tao Dade, after the actress filed for divorce in California.

None of the ten people were injured, police said.

The fire began sometime after 4 in the afternoon when an oven overheated, according to police. Doc Bird arrived soon after and immediately began rescuing each of the ten people trapped in the building.

Luckily for Doc Bird, and his back, eight of the ten people were females. You see while Doc Bird can fly, he doesn't possess any super powers.

"He was Superman to us," said Faye Raymond, one of the people saved.

And that's how most of this city feels about the fantastic Flying Man.

-END-

27

I was a hero again. I was back on top and it felt good. I wasn't the superstar I used to be, but that didn't matter. I no longer had to sing and dance for my supper. Now all I had to do was fly around until something happened.

It was while flying around and saving people that I first met Leticia. She was one of the many who were victims of crime while walking down the streets of the city. I first saw her when I heard her screaming down below. Wondering what had made her scream, I saw that her dress was torn and her arms empty.

"What seems to be the trouble, ma'am?" I asked her, swooping down to the sidewalk.

"Somebody stole my bag!" she shouted. "And then they knocked me down and tore my dress!"

I was immediately attracted to her eyes. They seemed to be glowing. They glowed like burning coals. I decided I wanted to get to know this woman, this victim of the city's streets.

"Let me take you to the hospital," I told her. "Let them check you out."

"Oh, I'm all right," she answered. "Just a few scratches and bruises."

"Let the doctors check you out," I replied. "Although from where I'm standing, you're looking mighty fine to me."

I looked at Leticia and she was smiling, a beautiful smile that could light up the centuries. "Oh, I bet you say that to all the women," she finally said. "I heard about you."

"It was all exaggeration and bullshit," I told her. "None of it was really very true."

"You knew all those girls, didn't you?" she said with a frown. "I mean, some of it had to be true."

"I knew a few of them," I finally admitted. "But none of them could compare with you. You have the nicest smile and eyes that I have ever seen. I mean, I think you're the best out of all those girls."

"My, oh my, how you can lie," she laughed. "You're that Doc Bird, the dude that can fly."

"That's me, all right. Would you like me to fly you out of here?"

"You don't see me protesting, do you, flying man?"

I picked her up and we went flying over the city of New York. It was a special flight, especially with Leticia. She seemed to be everything I ever wanted in a woman. She was attractive and smart, and had a good sense of humor. Yes, I sure did like Leticia from the first moment I met her.

"This is surely the best flight I've ever been on," Leticia told me. "You sure are something special, Doc Bird."

"Call me, Tommy," I said to her. "Everybody knows me as Tommy."

"Well, where are we headed, Tommy?"

"I thought I would take you to a nice spot I know."

"Is it close by because I didn't think I would be going a long way tonight."

"Oh, we'll be there in no time at all."

And then I took her to the Empire State Building. I flew up to the top of the tall skyscraper and landed below the spire.

"This is quite beautiful up here, Tommy," she said to me. "What an awesome view."

"I only come up here on special occasions," I told her.

"And this is a special occasion?"

"Yes, I think it is."

"Why, doctor Tommy, you trying to woo me or something?"

"Now how did you get that idea?"

"You're one bad cowboy, doc."

"I just think you're special, Leticia Holden."

"How many girls did you tell that to, doc?"

"No, I really think you're special, Leticia."

I then turned my head and kissed her. She was still holding on around my waist.

"Do you really mean it, Tommy?"

"Yes, Letty, darling, I really think I'm falling in love with you."

I kissed her again, and we sat there looking into each other's eyes thinking about where this relationship was going.

"Are you going to try to take advantage of me now, doc?" she suddenly asked me.

"No, I don't think I want to spoil this moment in any way," I told her. "I just want to remember your eyes and the magic of your lips."

"Oh, yes, Tommy, you are good," she finally said.

We sat up there looking at the city below, the millions of lights flickering in the distance. I wanted to make love to her, but I thought that we probably should wait. I didn't want to give her the wrong impression. She wasn't like the other girls I knew, she was someone I really wanted to get to know.

She wrapped her arms around my neck, and we flew off into the night. We soared above the lights and the people and the snarling vehicles below and I could see her beautiful smile and realized this was a night I would remember for a long time to come.

I finally landed in front of her apartment building, and with her arms still around me, we kissed passionately for several minutes. It was as if I was in love for the first time.

She branded herself into my heart, and then we kissed once again and we said good night. I watched her as she slowly walked to the door of her apartment building. I was mesmerized by her movement and by her voice.

"Good night, doc, I hope to see you again very soon," she said, disappearing inside.

Yes, a night to remember.

28

We're talking to Doc Bird—

You keep saving more and more people, doc. Are you ever going to stop?

Yes, I'll stop eventually. I'm just doing my part to make this a better place to live.

You talking about the planet?

Yes, I'm trying to make the planet a safer place to live.

Do you ever get lonely out there above the city, doc?

Not if all those tabloid reports are true. No, really, I get lonely, although I do have to say I met the most interesting person in my entire life while saving her.

Who is she, doc?

Well, her name is Leticia Holden, and I'm happy to say I'm going to ask her to marry me.

(Applause)

What makes her different than all the other girls, doc?

Well, I would have to say her eyes. Yes, her eyes are so lively and bright, like she can light up the entire world. And I would have to say her lips are soft and moist, like kissing a melted candle. But, most of all, her voice is full of energy and life like the laughter one hears on a warm summer day.

Beautiful, doc, really poetic. Have you taken her anywhere memorable?

Well, I did take her to the top of the Empire State Building. It was beautiful up there and being with Letty made it a memorable experience for me. I hope she would say the same.

Does anybody know about your marriage plans?

No, I'm announcing them here first. I thought you would appreciate the scoop. I'm going to take her to a pretty church I know of in California.

You heard it here first, folks, from the fabulous Doc Bird himself. Maybe now he'll tell us how he flies?

That will have to wait until I'm sure it's the right time.

Do you even have to flap your arms, doc?

No, gliding through the air is quite sufficient. I do need to flap my arms to gain speed, however.

And do you also have to eat like a bird?

Yes, you have to be very light to fly. You can't eat too much and put on excess weight. That won't allow you to float through the air.

Do you have anything else to say before we break for a commercial?

Peace is half a fist everyone.

Doc Bird everybody. We'll be back after this—

Doc Bird is tying the knot once again. That's what we hear and it's been confirmed by Doc Bird himself. Her name is Leticia Holden and she is certainly sweet.

But how much does Leticia know about Doc Bird and his many romances? We hear she knows a lot about everything that's gone on. But, my friends, Leticia, or Letty as she's called by her friends, has fallen in love with the fantastic Flying Man. That's right, head over heels in love.

Insiders say the marriage will be very soon and then Doc Bird is going fly her to some island. Who wouldn't like to be a fly on their wall?

This is, of course, the second marriage for Doc Bird. The first one falling apart after all the reports of his flying romances with an estimated 150 women. This guy really gets around. But insiders say he's ready to settle down with Leticia. We'll see about that, my friends.

Meanwhile, the happy couple reportedly flew to the top of the Empire State Building where they made delicious love. How about that love nest, my friends?

What's next for the flying couple? We don't know, but I'm sure it's going to be something good. Don't you think, my friends?

29

Letty was the only person on my mind all the time now. Whatever I did, wherever I went, I thought of her and her glowing brown eyes. I decided I would propose to her and then marry her in a big affair a few weeks later. There was no sense postponing for any length of time the only thing I really ever wanted to do besides flying.

That night, I flew to her apartment window and asked her to come fly with me. She was rather surprised, but willing.

I told her to wear something light, and then watched as she came out of the bathroom wearing a tight blouse and shorts. She looked fantastic, like the hottest babe on the planet. It was then I knew how lucky I was.

"Where are we going, flying man?" she asked, stepping toward the window.

"It's a surprise, my lovely Letty," I replied.

"Just get me back before morning," she said with a wicked smile.

Letty then came to the window and climbed on top of me. I was getting used to the excess weight of carrying people through the air, although every now and then those old fears of falling to the pavement appeared in my mind.

"Just sit back and enjoy the ride," I told her.

"Okay, superman, I'm all yours."

We laughed and talked about so many things as we flew through the air. A gentle breeze accompanied Letty's words as we made our way to the east.

"Are you flying me over the ocean, Tommy?" she suddenly asked.

"I was thinking about it," I replied with a smile.

"Just don't drop me, Tommy," she said. "I have a fear of being eaten."

"Don't worry, Letty, I'm the only one who will be eating you."

She laughed, and then we talked and talked and told each other how we felt about the scenery and the future.

"Land ho!" Letty finally shouted.

Yes, we were flying over land once again, and then we came to the city of London.

"Oh, Tommy, you've taken me to England," she squealed. "How romantic."

"Not just any place in London," I said to her. "But a place that suits a lady of your caliber."

And then down below, I spotted what I was looking for. I glided down to the roof and then placing my feet down, let Letty slide off my back.

"This is Buckingham Palace," she puffed. "What a beautiful place to fly to, Tommy."

"Well, you mean more to me than any monarch," I said. "Letty, I want you to be my queen."

Then, bending down on one knee, I presented her with a diamond ring. "Letty, will you be my queen forever more?"

She smiled that beautiful smile that always brightened my heart.

"I would be honored to be your queen, my darling Tommy," she finally said, placing the ring on her finger.

"Queen Victoria isn't fit to wash your feet, my Letty."

"Oh, Tommy, you always say the nicest things to me."

We kissed and kept on kissing until we fell to the roof and began making love. It was the best love session I had ever been involved. Letty's energy and verve made everything better. We twisted and turned and wrestled with our hips until the sun came up.

"Tommy, that was the best sex I've ever had," she said.

"It was pretty good for me too, my love."

"I really do feel like a queen."

"You're better than any queen."

"Tommy, I do love you."

"And I, Letty dear, love you."

I wished the night would never end. Just being there on top of Buckingham Palace with Letty my own queen was better than any dream I've ever had. We sat up there until mid-afternoon, and then when we were finally spotted by someone working at the palace, we flew off back to New York.

30

Doc Bird, the so-called Flying Man, married Leticia Holden today in a ceremony in New York. The wedding was by invitation only and the Flying Man didn't disappoint the crowds when he floated above the church and then glided down to the entrance.

This was the second marriage for Doctor Tommy Hagenhurst, who is divorced from his first wife, actress Tao Dade. That marriage ran into trouble when reports surfaced of the Flying Man having affairs with as many as 150 women.

There is no word whether the couple has a pre-nup agreement. It is said they will honeymoon on an island somewhere in the South Pacific.

After our wedding, I flew Letty to an island I knew of in the South Pacific. It was a small atoll with a sparkling lagoon and a nice sandy beach.

The only thing Letty was worried about was whether I was going to drop her in the ocean by mistake. Fortunately, we arrived safely.

"This is surely paradise, flying man," Letty said upon landing. "How come you never took me here before?"

"I was saving it for the right occasion."

"Well, I guess this is the right occasion, flying man."

We sat down on the beach, a blanket of snowy white sand, and immediately began making love. Letty and I were now married, and it felt wonderful to know we'd be together for the rest of our lives.

"Well, now that we're man and wife, I think you should know the secret of my unaided flight."

"I don't want to know, Tommy, if it's going to cause you any problems."

"No, I think it will just bring us closer together."

She smiled at me, that beautiful radiant smile, and then she climbed on my back and we flew back to America.

31

I flew Letty to my laboratory in south Florida. It was here I would prepare her to fly. It was a simple enough method involving our growing knowledge of genes, the basic unit of heredity in a living organism. I would genetically modify Letty's genes through a process called genetic transformation.

There was so much we were learning about genes and DNA. The possibilities were endless. Through genetic engineering, we could regenerate limbs, spine, and the brain. People now could be made smarter, faster, stronger, survive underwater longer, and even fly. Yes, it was all possible.

For example, if you wanted to regrow something, you would find a creature in Nature that was capable of doing it. The newt, for instance. Then after isolating the genes that make it happen, you insert those genes into the human body. It was now possible to transfer the whole block of genes into the person's body. The new genes are then incorporated into the human body and invade the host cells, inserting themselves into the genes of the cells. The product of all this is a human being who can regrow limbs and body parts.

After my own experimentation, I decided to implant the genes of various birds. Through the use of a gene gun, the new genes were incorporated into my body and flying was made possible. There was a definite transformation occurring as my body adapted to the new genes. First, my bones became lighter and then, my whole body seemed to reduce in weight. It was actually very interesting. I was now a GMO, a genetically modified organism. The whole process made me a chimera in genetic circles.

This was the process I was intending to use on Letty. I knew there were risks involved, but the benefits were well worth it. I talked everything over with Letty before proceeding with the modification. She agreed that the benefits made everything worthwhile.

The only thing she would have to endure was the gene gun or the biolistic particle delivery system. The technique I would use was simply referred to as bioballistics.

The gene gun is used to deliver DNA vaccines to human beings. It was quick and not really very painful.

"This is all I have to do, Tommy?" Letty said after I explained everything to her.

"Yes, darling, there's very little that can go wrong."

I intended to inject Letty with bird and newt genes so that she would be able to fly and also heal herself in case of an accident. Those are the same genes I injected into myself.

The gene gun injections went just as I planned and we waited until Letty's body began to adapt to the new genes. This was the genetic transformation.

It was a few days before Letty was ready to test her new body. She would start at several locations that weren't too high off the ground. If the preliminary testing went smoothly, we would see if she could fly at higher locations.

We began at the laboratory. I took Letty to the back and there we found a few wooden boxes. I would stack these boxes and then Letty would jump off.

"Okay, Letty darling, make sure you flap quickly and bend your knees," I told her. "Remember to float through the air."

"Okay, Tommy darling, I'll see you on Mount Everest."

We both laughed, and then Letty jumped off the boxes, flapped her arms wildly, and fell right down at my feet. Luckily, I broke her fall before she could really get hurt.

"That wasn't too bad," I said.

She looked up at me with a frown and then began to laugh. I laughed along with her.

"Is this how the Wright brothers started?" Letty asked.

"Actually, yes," I replied.

Laughing, I helped Letty back up the boxes. She tottered at the top and then jumped off once again. This time she made a mad scramble into the air, floated for a few seconds, and then came crashing down to the pavement. I was there again to help break her fall.

"Maybe it didn't work," she said with a grimace. "Maybe I'm just not made to fly."

"You should fly better than me, Letty darling," I said. "Women are much lighter than men, and if not too well developed, are perfectly balanced."

"Tell that to my body, my very heavy earth-bound body."

"You'll get the hang of it eventually."

Letty tried it several times with no luck. We were about to quit and try it another day when Letty suddenly bounded into the sky. She floated through the air, and began flapping her arms, when she began to fall. I was now flying right beside her, and immediately grabbed her.

"Aim your body upward," I told her.

That seemed to work, and soon Letty was flying high into the warm Florida air.

"Well, you're now as good as any bird, Letty darling."

"Oh, Tommy, and it's actually fun."

We made several flights that day. Letty almost crashed once. She suddenly bent her body the wrong way and went soaring down. I grabbed her on her way down, but she was so scared, we rolled around in the air and almost crashed into the pavement. At the last moment, however, I did take control and tragedy was averted.

On the last flight, Letty jumped from the roof, became unsteady, and then before I could help her, corrected herself and flew high into the blue sky of Florida. I was confident she was almost ready.

32

Doc Bird has a new flying companion. That's right, a woman believed to be Leticia Holden Hagenhurst, the Flying Man's wife, was seen flying over New York City with Doc Bird. She's the fantastic Flying Woman and she helped Doc Bird stop a robbery downtown today.

Witnesses said two men were robbing a drug store when Doc and Letty flew over the crooks and dropped metal disks on their heads. The two men were subsequently arrested by police.

"The flying woman dropped something on one of them," said a smiling Josa Lopez. "She did as well as the flying man."

A police spokesperson said help from Doc and Letty was appreciated, but that civilians should not involve themselves in police business.

The question most people are asking is if Doc Bird can teach his wife to fly, then is it possible for everyone to do it? Doc Bird, however, didn't stick around to answer any questions.

His wife, Letty, waved to everyone before flying off with her husband.

Yeah, I saw them, Nina. There was the flying man and the flying woman and they threw something metal down to stop the crooks. It was right here in front of my apartment building. The woman looked pretty slim. They say she's his wife. What a marriage that is, Nina.

MR. AND MRS. BIRD

By Ethan Faransky

What a couple!

Doc Bird and his wife, Letty, flew down from the heavens yesterday and prevented a robbery. They're better than the dynamic duo!

This Dyno Duo said they're out to make the world a safer place to live, never mind about dinner.

"I taught Letty how to fly," the fantastic Flying Man said. "But I'm not ready to give away the secret, yet."

The couple apparently flew up the coast from Florida where Doctor Tommy Hagenhurst's laboratory is located.

No one knows how the couple is able to fly. Doc Bird has vowed he would reveal the secret after accumulating enough money to live comfortably in the world.

Doctor Hagenhurst married Leticia Holden in a ceremony in New York a few weeks ago. They then spent their honeymoon on a South Pacific island. Doc Bird flew to the island carrying his wife the entire way. Talk about real love!

No word from the couple if they're going to continue to fight crime in the city. The potential crooks were arrested by police after trying to rob a drug store.

Doc Bird and JetLet, who his wife is now being called, soared down with metal disks to thwart the crime. They then flew off into the distance, arguing about who was going to make dinner.

There's no question about one thing: they are definitely the hottest couple in town right now!

-END-

We're talking to Doc Bird and JetLet—
How's your marriage going?

JETLET: It's going well, Rita.

DOC BIRD: You know what they say, the family that flies together, stays together.

And you're behaving yourself, doc?

DOC BIRD: Definitely, Rita. Letty is the best thing to ever happen to me.

(Applause)

Well, what happened to those crooks?

JETLET: They got what they deserved, Rita.

DOC BIRD: No one messes around in this city while Doc and Letty are taking care of it.

We hear Doc and Letty is out, everyone will be calling you Docticia. How about that?

JETLET: As long as they call us, Rita.

DOC BIRD: Yes, just call us.

You are a hot couple, Docticia, do you ever have any fights?

JETLET: Not really, Rita. Our marriage is something very special and we intend to keep it that way.

DOC BIRD: You got it. Nothing's going to get in the way of our love for each other.

One last question, who cooks dinner?

(Laughter)

JETLET: We both do to tell you the truth.

DOC BIRD: Yeah, my specialty is mac and cheese.

(Laughter)

Well, thanks, Docticia for stopping by to talk to us. We'll be back after these messages—

33

Everything was going well. I had learned to control that thing in my pants and now I saved all my love for Letty, I mean JetLet. Teaching her how to fly was probably the best thing I ever did. She now understood the freedom I felt when flying high in the air. For Letty, the experience seemed to redeem her soul. She was now loved and respected by many people, although none of them loved and respected her more than me.

We were some sort of crime-fighting team now, although nobody stepped forward to offer us any kind of remuneration. I had learned, however, that one could make a nice income with endorsements and book and TV deals. So Letty and I, Docticia to the public, kept on saving people hoping to cash in and make our lives a little easier.

We were in the midst of breaking up another robbery when one of the jerks fired their guns and a bullet hit me in the stomach. I crashed to the pavement, while Letty threw metal balls we had made at the crooks. She hit one of them, knocking him to the ground, while the other one got away.

"Are you hurt, Tommy?" I could hear Letty say in the midst of a great haze.

They then rushed me to the hospital, and I was wondering if I was going to be a goner.

I had forgotten all about my laboratory work, and then began wondering if that would eventually save me.

"Tommy, you just relax," I heard Letty say. "The doctor's going to be here any moment."

I looked down at the bullet wound, and then felt something strange happening. My stomach was going through rhythmic spasms, pushing the bullet up toward the hole. It felt like a soothing massage as my body slowly contracted and then relaxed. The bullet eventually came sliding out of the wound and fell to the cushion I was lying on.

When the doctor finally showed up, he marveled at how my body had apparently healed itself. He gasped when he found the bullet lying beside me.

"How did you do it?" he asked. "Your body seems to have regenerated."

"Yeah, well, that's my secret, doc," I said. "I'm sorry I took away your opportunity to open me up, but, hey, that's the med game."

I then sat up and smiled at Letty, who was standing next to my gurney.

"So then everything works, doc?" she said to me. "I mean, we didn't go down to Florida for the sunshine alone?"

I smiled, and then I jumped off the gurney and walked with Letty out of the hospital. I was happy the experiments had worked.

"You all right, doc?" the reporters asked as I walked with Letty outside.

"I'm fine, fine," I told them.

Then with Letty next to me, we jumped into the air and flew away to the west.

34

The bullet incident seemed to have caused Letty much concern. She insisted on talking about our mortality and age and suggested we begin thinking about having children. I was not adverse to the idea, but I cautioned Letty that once she was pregnant she could no longer fly. She thought about it and finally decided that we should adopt a few kids first, and then after a few years, try to have children ourselves.

I told her that adoption was a fine alternative and that we should choose children from various racial and ethnic backgrounds. Letty agreed, and we began searching for the right children immediately.

We heard about children in Africa who we could adopt. They came from poverty-stricken areas and we decided we could really change their lives and help the planet. We immediately flew to Somalia.

We met Asad shortly thereafter. He was eight years old and had lost both his mother and father. There was a strange twinkle in his eyes that immediately attracted both of us to him.

"Would you like to fly like the birds?" I asked him through an interpreter.

"Yes, I would like to fly far away from here and then come back and help my friends."

Letty and I both were affected by Asad's words. He seemed to want to help his people by first helping himself. That was something we were looking for in a child we would adopt.

We finally decided to adopt Asad, and carrying him, we flew him back to the United States. When we reached our home in New York, we immediately heard about children in New York's Harlem who were waiting to be adopted. We put Asad in the care of a nanny, and then went to see about those children.

We flew to an adoption agency in Harlem where the person in charge told us there were many deserving African-American children who were waiting for adoption. That's when we met Keisha, a seven-year-old girl with a glowing smile and kind, intelligent eyes.

"How would you like to come live with us?" Letty asked her.

"Only if you think I wouldn't be an unnecessary burden," she replied.

The two of us melted at the remark, and we decided we would adopt Keisha.

"Do you think you could get along with an older brother and many more brothers and sisters to come?" I asked her.

"Yes, I would do anything to make you happy," she replied.

We knew Keisha was right for us from the very first moment we met her. She was everything one could hope for in a child and it was a miracle she hadn't been adopted before we came. But Keisha was still there and was soon our new daughter.

We flew her back to our home in New York's suburbs and were happy to see her take an immediate liking to Asad. Our new family was beginning to take shape, although we had only just started.

"I want a big family, Tommy," Letty said. "Oh, it will make me so very happy."

"Then you shall have one," I told her. "I want to make all your dreams come true, Letty darling."

35

We're talking celebrity adoptions and we have with us Docticia—
Stick around, y'all—
First, let's bring out Docticia and their first adopted child, Asad—
(Applause)
DOC BIRD: Thank you, Opal. It's great being here.
JETLET: Yes, thank you for having us on the show. I want to introduce all of you to Asad. He comes from Somalia and we adopted him after meeting him there.
Does he speak any English?
JETLET: A little, but we brought along an interpreter who will help us. Ask him anything you want.
Are you happy living with Docticia?
(Laughter and applause)
ASAD: I'm not sure I know who you mean.
(Laughter)
ASAD: But my parents are very nice and I'm glad to be with them all the time.
(Applause)
What was your life like in Somalia, Asad?
ASAD: It was terrible. We didn't have anything to eat or drink and slept in dirt and filth. It was really very bad.
When did you first meet Doc Bird and JetLet?
ASAD: Are those my parents you are referring to?
Yes, Asad, your Mom and Dad—
ASAD: I first met them a few months ago in Somalia. I was very glad to see them.
You knew they were your new parents?

ASAD: Some woman came to our village and told me all about them. I was very excited to see them very soon after that.

Did you know your parents could fly?

ASAD: That I did not know until later.

What do you think about their flying?

ASAD: I think it is, what is the term? Awesome.

Well, introduce us to your next child, JetLet—

JETLET: Our next child is Keisha. She came from an agency in Harlem in New York and she's so intelligent and pleasant it's just amazing we found her when we did.

Hello, Keisha, are you happy with your Mom and Dad?

KEISHA: They are truly the best people on the planet. I'm very happy, Opal, and I just want to tell everyone how much I love both of them.

(Applause)

Do you want to fly, Keisha?

KEISHA: Yes, ever so much. Mom and Dad fly with me all the time. It's a wonderful feeling and truly amazing.

Did Dad say he will teach you?

KEISHA: Oh yes, Opal. He tells me all the time.

DOC BIRD: I just want to say, Opal, that flying is something that might become a part of my family in the future.

Are you going to teach them, doc?

DOC BIRD: Probably.

How about the rest of us, doc?

DOC BIRD: That will probably happen in the future, too.

It's so good to have all of you with us today. Docticia, everybody, and their family. We'll be back after this—

36

The next thing Letty and I wanted to do was go to the Middle East and see what we could do for peace in that region. We flew to the area and made sure the people down below spotted us. Then we soared down to the ground and decided we would find out about adopting an Israeli. It took us a long time, but we finally ended up meeting Isaac.

Isaac was only interested in how we were able to fly. I told him it was a secret and he immediately smiled and told us that we should keep it a secret from people who wanted to commit violence. I asked Isaac if he was interested in peace in the area.

"Oh, yes, it is the only thing we really want," he told us. "I think your flying can help bring peace."

I smiled at him. "Yes, if used properly and at the right time," I replied. "How about you, Isaac, would you want to fly?"

"Oh, yes, I would like to fly and help everyone live in peace."

We liked Isaac right away, and he told us his name in Hebrew was Yitzhak. I didn't know much Hebrew, but Isaac told us he would be very glad to teach us.

We adopted Isaac and then flew him back to the United States, where we introduced him to his new brother and sister, Asad and Keisha. But we weren't finished.

After leaving Isaac with Asad and Keisha, Letty and I flew back to the Middle East. We finally landed in Syria. The Syrians were quite taken with our ability to fly and continued to ask us for the secret. I told them I would tell everybody the secret in due time, but first I wanted to adopt one of their people.

We soon met Ishmael. He was about the same age as Isaac, about seven years old, and about as tall. We thought he would be a good person to add to our growing family, and one who could be a good friend to Isaac.

"Are you interested in peace, Ishmael?" I asked him.

"Oh yes, I think it is very important for people to live together without any violence," he said.

We were very taken with Ishmael's words, and we decided we would like to adopt him and bring him back to the United States.

"Will you tell us the secret at that time?" one Syrian asked us.

"Something like that," I told him.

Anyway, I flew Ishmael back to America with Letty flying right beside me. When we arrived, we immediately introduced Ishmael to Isaac. They immediately got along with each other.

"I did not know so much about your country," Ishmael said. "But I do know we don't have to be enemies."

"Yes, we will be good friends until the end of time," Isaac replied. "Your people are related to my people and have been for centuries."

Because everybody was getting along with each other so well, I decided we would fly down to Florida and give them all the power to fly. This time, I wouldn't use the gene gun, but a simple syringe. I was confident this method would be just as effective in bringing about the desired results.

"You mean we will all be flying?" asked Ishmael, after I told the family my plan.

"Yes, I want to see the whole family fly," I told him.

"It will surely be the greatest day in my life," said Isaac.

"It will be the greatest day in all of our lives," agreed Keisha.

"I will fly like a bird and help my family and friends," said Asad.

I hoped giving them all the ability to fly would reinforce their love for each other. That, I believed, was the most important thing we could have. I wanted the family to really love one another and be kind to each other. That was all a family really needed in my opinion. Letty agreed with me and thought giving them all the power to fly was a good idea.

I began with carrying Asad, while Letty carried Keisha. We flew down to the Florida laboratory, and then I returned for Isaac. Letty and Keisha remained in Florida. After flying Isaac to the laboratory, I returned to New York for Ishmael.

When the whole family was gathered in Florida, I took each of them to the lab room and injected them with the genetic solution.

"This is so exciting," said Asad. "I feel I can't wait."

"I already see feathers growing out of you, Asad," smiled Isaac. "You will be a bird in no time at all."

"And you, my friend, will soon lay an egg," laughed Ishmael.

"That's a good yolk, Ishey," said Keisha. "A real feather in your cap."

They all started laughing, and after a few moments, I thought they were ready to try to fly. Asad was first. We put him on top of an old oil barrel and told him to jump off and flap his arms.

"I will be happy to be a bird," he said, before climbing up onto the barrel.

He then did everything we told him to do, and he jumped into the air. He flapped his small arms and drifted up into the air.

"I am flying!" he shouted.

Everyone began applauding his effort, until he suddenly shifted his weight and dropped to the ground.

We all ran to see if he was all right, and then when we reached Asad, he looked up at us and smiled.

"I'm glad you're not injured," I said to him. "I told you all that you have to be careful."

We took Asad back to the oil barrel and told him to try again.

"I will be very careful this time," he said, standing on top of the barrel. "I really do want to fly."

The second time, Asad jumped into the air, and flapping his arms, began to fly high into the sky. He had done it.

"Well, that makes three of us now," I said to Letty. "It's really not as hard as it looks."

"No, I think you are right, Tommy, the whole world can really do it if given the secret," she said.

"Yes, but I don't think I'll tell them for a while," I replied. "I want our family to enjoy it first."

Keisha was next. I was interested to see if it was any harder for a girl to fly. For Keisha, it was rather easy. She started to fly the moment she jumped into the air.

"It feels great," she shouted to us down below. "The greatest feeling ever."

"Well, don't fly too high, darling," I said to her. "Your wings may melt."

I was, of course, thinking of the story of Icarus, who was given wax wings by his father, Daedalus, and then flew too close to the sun, melting the wings, and sending him crashing to earth. Thinking about the story renewed my fears that something could happen to one of my family members.

"You have to let them soar, Tommy," Letty finally said. "Nothing you say will keep them chained to the ground."

Letty was right, as she always was, that I had to let them be free and let whatever happened to happen.

Isaac was next. He was so excited about flying that he slipped off the oil barrel as soon as he climbed up. He laughed, and then he hoisted himself back up and began flying right away.

"Tov meod!" I shouted to him in Hebrew. It meant, very good.

He smiled at me and continued to flap his arms and soar into the sky. That made five of us able to fly. The last one to try to do it was Ishmael.

"I will fly higher than the pyramids," he said with a smile.

Ishmael then climbed up on the oil barrel, and jumping off, soared into the blue sky.

"Well, that's all of them, Letty, darling," I said. "I think we should join them and then show them a few things."

We then all jumped into the air, the entire family, and began flying in the clear blue sky. Keisha and Ishmael particularly enjoyed the flight, laughing the entire time.

"It is good to be a bird," Ishmael said happily. "I think it is the best feeling on earth."

"Or off it," said Isaac.

The six of us really enjoyed ourselves that day we all learned to fly. But it was springtime, and I thought it would be more exciting if we went north to New York. The Big Apple would never be the same once it was introduced to Doc Bird and his flying family. I was really looking forward to it.

37

An armed robbery was foiled today by Doc Bird and his flying family—

Here's a report from Tom Tyler—

They swooped out of the sky, all six of them, to prevent an armed robbery from taking place down below. That's right, all six of them. They're the flying family of Doc Bird and JetLet.

"We saw the kids swoop down and throw metal balls at the crooks." And Peggy Sewell was not the only one to witness the heroes in action.

"All of them flew right out of the sky and attacked those men. There were three little boys and one girl."

Those were the words of May Hoover, one of many who watched the Doc Bird family prevent the armed robbery.

It is not known if the family will remain in the Big Apple to fight crime since none of the family members are talking.

The police, meanwhile, were thankful, yet cautious. "It's not police policy for civilians to help make arrests," one spokesperson said.

The Hagenhursts, however, had already flown away. This is truly a story that's really for the birds.

Tom Tyler, World News, New York.

Click to watch video

This is my flying family ready to help anyone in distress. I'm Doc Bird. This is my wife, Letty or JetLet. This is Asad. He's from Somalia. This is Keisha. She's from Harlem. This is Isaac. He's from Israel. And this is

Ishmael. He's from Syria. That is my family. Doc Bird's flying family. That's right, all of us can fly! We're here to save you from any problem you might have. See you!

END of video

38

Letty told me the family needed to be bigger. She wanted representatives of every culture and faith in our flying family, and I agreed. So we gathered our family members together and told them we would be flying to the Orient.

"I would like a little Chinese brother or sister," said Keisha with a wide grin. "It would be very pleasant."

"Yes, the family would only get smarter," said Isaac. "They are very skilled at many things."

With that settled, we all flew off to China. It was a long trip, and I had received some information on where to go to adopt a little Chinese child. We finally made it to Beijing, and asked for directions to the agency arranging for the adoption.

The problem, of course, was that none of us could speak Chinese. We were stumbling around when a young boy came up to us and showed us where the agency was. He said his name was Ka-Ching and that he knew a little English because his mother had taught him, but then she had died and he was on his own.

We immediately asked Ka-Ching if he would like to join our family. He smiled and said, "It would be my pleasure."

We asked him where he was living, and he told us on the streets of Beijing. He slept wherever he could find a place to sleep for a few hours. Then Letty took his hand, and told him he would sleep in a warm bed from now on. Ka-Ching smiled and said that would be good.

"It would be pleasant to sleep well," he said.

"You can share my room," said Asad. "We will have much to talk about."

Then I picked up little Ka-Ching and we flew off into the sky. Ka-Ching was amazed.

"I didn't know you could do it," he said. "Maybe you will teach me."

"Yes, we will, little Ka-Ching."

We decided that before going home, we would go to Japan. We told our family members, and Ka-Ching immediately volunteered to direct us to the island country.

There was an agency there that I knew about, and I decided we would all fly there and try to adopt a girl. The family was growing bigger, but so far, we had four boys and only one girl.

When we finally landed at the agency, everyone standing on the street was surprised at our ability to fly. They only wanted to know if it was possible for them to fly, too.

"In time, my good people," I told them. "I will soon tell everyone my secret of flying."

The Japanese at the agency spoke English, and they told us they had a little girl who would be glad to be part of our growing family.

"Her name is Kishi, which means 'a long and happy life,'" the woman at the agency said. "She will be very happy to meet you."

When we first saw Kishi, we couldn't believe how beautiful she was. She had glowing almond eyes and a pretty smile, and was wearing a red kimono.

"I am very happy to see all of you," she said, after being introduced to the family. "I like you all very much."

"And we like you, Kishi," I said. "How would you like to come and live with us?"

"It would be ever so much fun," she replied, with that pretty smile of hers. "I would like that ever so much."

I looked at Letty, and she nodded her approval. It was impossible not to like Kishi. She was beautiful and quite adept at speaking English. I wanted to make her part of the family almost from the moment I laid eyes on her.

"She is most beautiful," said Ka-Ching. "I will like her very much."

"We all will like her, Ka-Ching," Keisha replied. "And I will have one pretty sister."

"I will be most honored," said Kishi. "I will like a sister ever so much."

We adopted Kishi and Letty flew her back to America while I took care of Ka-Ching. Flying back with him in my arms, I asked Ka-Ching if he was ready to fly.

"As ready as having been born with wings," he replied.

When we reached Florida, I injected both Kishi and Ka-Ching with the genetic solution, and they were soon flying with the rest of the family. We were now a family of eight, a family that was still growing and still kings and queens of the sky.

39

This just in to our newsroom—

Doc Bird and his flying family began helping victims of the Haitian earthquake by flying them to other islands and the United States.

The Fantastic Flying Clan consists of six children and Doc Bird and JetLet, Tommy Hagenhurst and his wife, Letty. All of the family members can fly, and they did their best to transport earthquake victims to other areas.

"We're just doing our part to help out in this terrible tragedy," said Doctor Hagenhurst. "We'd even like to adopt some of the victims."

The Hagenhursts did end up adopting one of the Haitian girls they saved, a six-year-old named Orva. They didn't say where they were flying the little girl and whether they would be teaching her to fly.

"Right now there are more important things we must do," said Letty Hagenhurst. "We really want to help the people of Haiti in these sad and terrible times."

The Hagenhursts were part of the enormous relief effort to help Haitians who were left starving and homeless from the 7.0-magnitude quake. The quake also left thousands dead and injured.

"Everyone should help out in their own way," said Doc Bird, the so-called Fantastic Flying Man. "If we all work together, we can make this a better planet and help those who need to be helped."

Now let's go to our reporter in Port-au-Prince, Reggie Burke—

I'm standing here on the ground in Port-au-Prince while all around us the Doc Bird family flies through the skies of Haiti. They're doing their part to help in the quake crisis.

Standing with me is the mother of the Fantastic Flying Clan, JetLet Hagenhurst.

How is the relief effort going?

There's a lot of damage and a lot of dead, Reggie. We're doing our best to help out in Haiti's hour of need.

How many people have you flown to other islands?

Many. We are just doing our part in this very real and very sad crisis.

How long will you be with the relief effort?

Until the job is finished, Reggie. We're not going to leave Haiti until the situation has been stabilized.

And what about the little girl you decided to adopt?

Her name is Orva and she is a beautiful addition to our growing family. We found her in the rubble where her mother and father died. It was really a tragic situation, and so, we thought we would help out by adopting her. She really is a beautiful little girl.

Will you teach her to fly?

Yes, we will, Reggie. She'll become a necessary part of our expanding family.

Thank you very much, JetLet—

Well, that's the situation right now in Port-au-Prince. There is rubble and dead bodies and starving people in the streets, but people like Doc Bird's flying family give them hope for the future. Reggie Burke reporting—

40

We have the Doc Bird Fantastic Flying Clan with us today so stick around, y'all—
OPAL

Hello, everybody, let's welcome that Fantastic Flying Clan, everybody!

Here's Doc Bird, the Fantastic Flying Man, and his wife, JetLet, Letty Hagenhurst, and their ten adopted children—

Okay, here's Asad, from Somalia; Keisha, from Harlem in New York; Isaac, from Israel; Ishmael, from Syria; Ka-Ching, from China; Kishi, from Japan; Orva, from Haiti; Amba, from India; Masood, from Nigeria, and Sarito, from Spain. They are the Fantastic Flying Clan, ladies and gentlemen!

(Applause)

So how y'all doing? JetLet?

We're all doing just fine, Opal. We're happy to be here.

Now, let's see, there are 12 in your family now. Is that right? And you're talking about adding more to that?

JETLET: That's right, Opal. We don't think 12 is enough.

(Laughter)

JETLET: No, we seriously want to add more kids to our family and help them realize their dreams. And as you can see, we're going to definitely have at least one more because I'm pregnant.

(Applause)

Doc Bird, are you all right with this?

DOC BIRD: Of course, Opal. Letty and I have discussed it many times and we feel that we're only helping ourselves in helping others. We have the money and resources to do it, so hey, why not?

That's a lot of mouths to feed—

DOC BIRD: Sure is, Opal. But when you look at these amazing faces, don't you think it's worth it?

What do you say, everybody?

(Applause)

Worth it!

ISAAC: We certainly agree that it's worth it.

(Laughter)

KEISHA: We don't eat that much.

(Laughter)

Aren't they all just adorable, y'all?

So what does the family think about saving people and flying through the air? We'll ask them after we come back. The Fantastic Flying Clan, everybody!

(Applause)

Let's bring them out, the Doc Bird Flying Family—

(Applause)

There are 12 of you, is that correct? You are from countries from all over the world and you all can fly, isn't that right? How do you do it?

DOC BIRD: We stick together and really care for each other.

Show us how you fly. The little one, Kishi, from Japan. Let's see you fly—

(Applause)

Unbelievable. Look at her fly around the studio. It is really quite extraordinary and all of you can do it, isn't that right?

KEISHA: Quite correct, Louis. We're birds of a feather who fly together.

(Applause)

And do you do everything like a bird?

KA-CHING: Oh yes, do you want to see me make a nest in your hair?

Great.

SARITO: Do you want to see me lay an egg? I can lay an egg—

Can you?

SARITO: Only kidding.

ISAAC: She can't really lay an egg, but I can.

We'll be right back with the Doc Bird Flying Family. Stay right where you are, everybody--

41

Letty was pregnant, there was no doubt of that. She had first told me in the spring and now it was almost Christmas again. Her belly was as round and plump as Santa's. This pleasant fact gave me the idea to actually be Santa for Christmas. I would be able to be the closest thing to the jolly old St. Nick since the world began. First of all, I could fly. Second of all, I knew the secret of flying without mechanical assistance. These two factors could help me recreate Santa without many problems.

The first thing I had to do was find reindeer. I took along a syringe of the bird gene solution, and then with all of my boys, flew up to Canada. We soon located some reindeer in the hills of the Northwest Territories. I still was not sure what would happen after I injected the reindeer with the genetic solution. I brought along reins just in case the reindeer decided to take off into the clear, blue skies.

Thor was one of the boys we found in Scandinavia. He knew something about reindeer and would assist me in trying to teach the creatures what to do. When we spotted the reindeer down below, we swooped down and landed as gently as possible, trying not to scare them. It was no use. They immediately ran off the moment we landed.

We chased the reindeer pack for several miles, until they finally halted and we landed beside them.

"This isn't going to hurt, big guy," I said, injecting one of them with the genetic solution.

The reindeer, bearing huge antlers, began coughing and heaving. Not knowing what else to do, I jumped on his back and wrapped my arms around his huge neck. The reindeer, becoming alarmed, began charging up a hill. I hung on for dear life, and then, when he reached the summit of the hill, he made a great leap and jumped into the air and streaked into the sky.

I hung on. I then began screaming, although I could have jumped off at any point and flown myself to safety. I didn't think of that at the time, however, and kept screaming.

Well, the reindeer we eventually named Comet took me on quite a ride that day. It felt like I was riding a comet. He must have flown from northern Canada to southern Canada and back again ten times. Eventually, however, he calmed down and I began feeding him food pellets I had brought along. He liked the pellets immensely.

We flew back to Florida that day with nine reindeer. One of them even had a rather large red nose. The children loved playing with the reindeer and flying them through the whispering air. When we finally arrived, a sleigh was waiting for us near our home in Florida. I had contracted with someone to build it to my specifications and I was not disappointed. The only thing left to do was to hitch the reindeer. When we finally did that, a few of us jumped into the sleigh and soared off into the sky. For the first time in human history, there really was a Santa who could fly. Getting down the chimneys would be up to the kids. But before we could really find out if it would all work out, we had a Christmas special to do. The money we would earn from that would fund the Santa experiment.

42

Live from Hollywood, this is the Fantastic Flying Clan's Christmas Special—

Starring Doc Bird, the Fantastic Flying Man, and JetLet, Letty Hagenhurst.

And what about the rest of the family?

I'm Asad. I'm from Somalia.

I'm Keisha. I'm from New York.

I'm Isaac. I'm from Israel.

I'm Ishmael. I'm from Syria.

I'm Ka-Ching. I'm from China.

I'm Kishi. I'm from Japan.

I'm Orva. I'm from Haiti.

I'm Amba. I'm from India.

I'm Masood. I'm from Nigeria.

I'm Sarito. I'm from Spain.

I'm Thor. I'm from Norway.

I'm Minowa. I'm a Native American.

We're Jimmy and Jane, we're twins from Missouri.

I'm Zorya. I'm from Hungary.

I'm Shannon. I'm from Ireland.

I'm Duy. I'm from Vietnam.

I'm Sook. I'm from Korea.

I'm Julio. I'm from Mexico.

I'm Michael. I'm from Canada.

I'm Jelani. I'm from Russia.

I'm Gabriela. I'm from Argentina.

I'm Acar. I'm from Turkey.

I'm Joaquim. I'm from Brazil.

And I'm Rapa from Hawaii. My name means moonbeam.

And those are the members of the Fantastic Flying Clan!

(Applause)

DOC BIRD: And now we'd like to do a song for all of you. From all of us, the Doc Bird Flying Family—

JETLET: No, we discussed that, doc. It's now the Fantastic Flying Clan.

DOC BIRD: Oh, well. I liked the other name better.

AMBA: Oh, Dad.

It's a merry merry Christmas
A merry Christmas for me
It's a merry merry Christmas
A merry Christmas to see

And it's a merry merry Christmas
A merry Christmas to be
Yes, it's a merry merry Christmas
And a time to be free.

Here comes Christmastime again
Laughing all the way
Here comes Christmastime, my friend
Snow falling through the day.

And it's a merry merry Christmas
A merry Christmas to be
Yes, it's a merry merry Christmas
And a time to be free.

Here comes Christmastime again
Laughing all the way
Here comes Christmastime, my friend
Snow falling through the day.

And it's a merry merry Christmas.

(Applause)
Merry Christmas everybody!
ISAAC: And Happy Chanukah to all!
So come on and light a candle
Burning through time
Yes, come on and light a candle
Watching them shine.

O Chanukah, O Chanukah
A festival of lights
O Chanukah, O Chanukah
Such a peaceful delight.

ISAAC: Thank you everyone and here's wishing everybody peace
wherever they may live.
  KISHI: And we'll be right back
  MINOWA: After these important messages—

SOOK: It's good to be back with all you wonderful people.
JELANI: Here's another song we sing.
SHANNON: Enjoy.

Dancing
Papers flying in the park
Dancing
Flowers swaying in the dark
Dancing
Reasons sailing out to sea
Dancing
Loving you you're loving me

And when you're stepping
Your shoes fall gently
And now you're dancing with me
Dance together
Our love forever

And keep on dancing with me.

Dancing
Our bodies moving with the flow
Dancing
A summer breeze that never knows
Dancing
Sunshine cutting through the storm
Dancing
Or maybe trying to keep warm

And when you're dancing
Your shoes fall gently
And now you're dancing with me.
Dance together
Our love forever
And keep on dancing with me.

Dancing
La la la la la la la la
Dancing
La la la la la.

KISHI: Hey Keisha, why are stadiums so cold all the time?
KEISHA: Maybe because there are fans in every seat.
KISHI: You are correct, O knowing one.
KEISHA: That's me all right. Now let me ask you one. Why did the little girl throw her clock out the window?
KISHI: She wanted to see time fly.
KEISHA: O knowing one.
KISHI: O knowing one.
ISAAC: While they're complimenting themselves, we'll look at these commercial messages—

JIMMY: Hey, Jane, do you know why spiders are so good at baseball?
JANE: Spiders, yech.
JIMMY: Yes, but why are they so good at baseball?

JANE: Yech, Jimmy.
JIMMY: Because they're used to catching flies.
JANE: Yech. That's the most awful riddle I have ever heard.
JIMMY: Yeah, it was pretty good, wasn't it?

GABRIELA: And now here's another song—

I know you think I'm crazy
You said I could be wrong
You disregard the sadness
And say that we'll get along.

I say there's too much hatred
You say I look too close
When I see people struggling
You say, yes, so are most.

Everyone is thinking money
So what else can I do?
And though the times are filled with trouble
Still I'll get along with you.

So let the whispers echo
Past realms of solemn blue
For if the world should crumble
Still I'll get along with you.

Yeah, I'm going to get along with you...

Everyone is bleeding, honey
So what else can I do?
And though the darkness swells before me
Still I'll get along with you.

Oh, get along everyone!

I'm going to get along with you...

43

The Santa thing didn't go well. I tried to become this mythological character that they say is somewhat based on truth and found the whole idea was absurd. The world expected this character to give away presents for free, do it happily, and give away the gifts to everyone in the world in only one night. Totally ridiculous.

The problem was I didn't want to disappoint the children – mine as well as everyone else's. No, against my better judgment, we hitched nine of the reindeer to the sleigh, piled in as many presents as we could in a big red sack, and then prepared ourselves for a trip around the world in only one night. The children were very enthusiastic about such an endeavor. They promised they would stick close to the sleigh and accompany me on my trip. There were now 50 of us in the family, so I decided I might as well try.

So after the Christmas special, we made our final preparations. Letty decided she would come along despite the fact that Mrs. Claus always waited at home for Santa to return. Letty told me this was a new age in which women could do almost as much as a man, maybe more. She wouldn't stay at home while her whole family was out trying to make a myth come true. She was coming along with everybody else, she informed me.

The only problem was that Letty was very pregnant. I didn't want to take the chance that she would have the baby while we were gone, so I told her to bundle up and sit in the sleigh. If anything happened, I could fly her back to a hospital.

So the day before Christmas, about 10 in the morning, I walked out to the sleigh and jumped in with Letty. The rest of the family joined me in the shining light determined to make mythology come true. We decided we would start with Australia and then work our way west to Japan and China. We would then fly to Asia and Europe and Africa and then back to the United States and Central and South America. It was quite a trip we had planned, and I doubted whether we would or should make it.

The children, however, were all for it. They didn't know what they were really getting themselves into. I tried explaining the logistics to them, but they refused to listen. They were like most of the children on the planet who happily follow this myth of the ages without really thinking about what it truly entails.

Anyway, the morning before Christmas we started off. We flew west over the United States until we reached the Pacific Ocean. There were lots of tiny islands here and we began by swooping down and throwing presents to anyone standing down below. The people seemed delighted with our visit, and so, we moved on.

We reached Australia later that day. It was already dark and we began landing on several roofs to deliver the presents. The children, who were flying beside us, grabbed presents and flew off to other chimneys and houses. In this way, we could take care of several houses at a time.

The younger children went down the chimneys and delivered the presents to the individual houses. The problem, however, was that we were running out of presents. We hadn't even completed Australia and there were only a few presents left.

"Can't we go back and get more?" asked one of the children.

"No way," I replied, "this little stunt has cost me enough money as it is."

"But what about the children?"

It was that absurd myth once again. Everyone gets a free gift around the world. Who really could afford such a venture? You would have to be God Himself, and still the details were ridiculous.

I decided to take the few presents we had remaining back to the United States and give them to the children there. It was our home, after all, and I felt they kind of deserved some presents after all the money I had made by myself and with the family. So, before finishing Australia, we packed up and went back to America. We arrived in the middle of the night, and decided to begin leaving presents in the Northeast and work our way west.

We set up the same system with the children flying down the chimneys and the sleigh landing on several rooftops. But after doing many houses in Massachusetts, New York, and New Jersey, the presents finally ran out. It was an impossible task, and all of us soon realized the folly of the undertaking.

The only positive was that Letty didn't go into labor. She sat there, round and bloated, and helped as best she could. In the end, the myth was too much for us to carry out. There wasn't enough money to buy everything for everybody and there never would be. Santa would have to remain a myth for the very young.

44

The Doc Bird Flying Family did their part for the children of the world. World News has learned it was Doc Bird playing Santa Claus as he and a sleigh of presents, accompanied by his wife and his 50 children, flew to parts of the world and distributed presents to the children and families during the night. The doc even helped nine reindeer to actually fly through the air pulling the huge sleigh. Here's Bob Gates—

'Twas the night before Christmas and all through the house, not a creature was stirring, not even a mouse. Well, maybe there were some creatures stirring from the Hagenhurst family.

That's right, while the children slept, Doc Bird and his flying family of 50 left presents for one and all in Australia and the United States. Well, only select parts because, you see, the family ran out of presents.

"We tried our best," said a solemn Doc Bird, Tommy Hagenhurst. "But it was just too expensive and too large a venture."

At least, they tried to do Santa's work.

"We ran out of presents," said Shannon Hagenhurst. "That was the only problem."

"But what a problem," added Isaac Hagenhurst, one of the many flying children.

Well, at least they're left with nine flying reindeer. "I don't know what we're going to do with the reindeer," said Doc Bird. "I guess we have to keep them."

Meanwhile, many children in Australia and the United States ended up with gifts, courtesy of the Hagenhurst flying clan.

And is Doc Bird now going to buy presents for his family of wife, Letty, and 50 children?

"It's going to be a quiet Christmas," he would only say.
The rest of the clan is a bit more enthusiastic.
"Merry Christmas to all and to all a good night!"
Bob Gates reporting—

45

It was time for Letty to have her baby. It was New Year's Eve, the dawn of another year, and Letty was in pain. I called the doctor and then holding her hand, we flew to the hospital with 20 of our children trailing behind.

Things went smoothly at the hospital and then, at exactly 12 midnight, Letty had her baby. He was a beautiful boy with Letty's glowing brown eyes. There was an intelligent look to this new addition to our family, and I immediately wanted to name him Edison. Letty lovingly approved the choice and the baby was now known as Edison Holden Hagenhurst. I was ecstatic. This was my first child who carried my genes and I tried not to show that I would favor this little baby over the 50 other children in my family.

"He sure is beautiful," Keisha said, upon seeing Edison for the first time. "My new baby brother."

I thanked Keisha for her remarks, and then immediately turned my attention to Letty. "How are you feeling, darling?" I asked. "You did a quite wonderful job, my dear Letty."

Letty smiled at me. She had worked hard to produce this new member of the family and it showed on her tired face.

Isaac looked at Edison and smiled. "You'll be flying in no time, my little bro," he said.

I wanted to laugh. I began thinking, however, at what age I would allow the baby to fly. This was a decision I would talk over with Letty, I finally decided. I mean at what age do you allow a baby to fly? It isn't a question one asks himself all the time.

The main thing was that Letty was all right and the baby was healthy. Anything else really didn't matter to me. I was feeling really good, really good, when the doctor told me everything was fine. I now had a child of my own to spoil and teach and be proud of. Not that I didn't love the 50 children we had already adopted, each one of them was very special to me and would remain so no matter what. But I was looking forward to getting to know little Edison. He would be very special to me for the rest of my life.

"Edison very strong and healthy, father," Ka-Ching was saying. "He will be our Superman."

I looked at Ka-Ching and smiled.

46

Live from Hollywood, it's the Doc Bird and JetLet Show—
Starring Tommy and Letty Hagenhurst and their fantastic flying clan of 75—
Today's guests are Jim McGrand and Lola Stack—
And now here's Doc Bird and JetLet—

Hi everybody and welcome to today's show. My fantastic flying clan can do more than fly. Just take a listen—

Oh, Honeybunch
Do you need a little hand?
Oh, Honeybunch
Can I be your little man?
And there we'll sit
Together side by side
Oh, Honeybunch.

A smiling face is all we need today
And every day
Our love will melt away.

Oh, Honeybunch
Do you think our love will grow?
Oh, Honeybunch
Do you think our love will know?
Just why we are
So happy side by side
Oh, Honeybunch.

A dreamy place is all we need today
And all our days
Our love will melt away.

Oh, Honeybunch.

A smiling face is all we need today
And every day
Our love will melt away.

Oh, Honeybunch.

Thank you, thank you. We'll be back after these messages—

It's so good to be back on national television, don't you think so, Letty, dear?
The only problem is who is going to take care of the baby? That's right, the baby. Have you met our new baby, Edison?
Let's bring him out—
Hello, Edison, here's daddy—
EDISON: Mama.
Well, isn't that a surprise?
And now, Letty dear, won't you join me for a song?
Delighted, doc.

It's only natural
For you to be with me
And through the love we share
We'll make it naturally

All the reasons
Through the seasons
Time after time again.

It's only natural
For our love to be
And we will always care

For one another naturally

All our questions
And confessions
Time after time again.

It's only natural
For love is all we need
And through the coming years
We'll be together naturally

It's only natural.

Thank you very much everyone. We'll be back with our very special guests after these important messages, so stick around—

47

Edison was growing all the time. He was a little baby for only a short time. He would crawl around and get in everyone's way, until somebody, usually one of the girls, would pick him up and put him in the playpen. We were one big happy family. It was true. Letty was happier than ever before and so was I. The rest of the family seemed to sense our renewed spirit and seemed to be happier because of it. This was a time when everyone began stressing the positive in their lives. Whenever something negative occurred, we would try to change the situation to a positive one.

Letty and I stopped our flying and crime-fighting to take care of Edison full-time and avoid distractions or possible injuries. The family, meanwhile, was still growing. We still felt as if we would enjoy adopting someone from another culture who was less fortunate than we were. The candidates never ran out. One day we were adopting someone from Vietnam and the next, someone from Bolivia. Like I said, the list of possible candidates never ran out. The family swelled to 100 as we cared for Edison. He was the only one of our children that we raised from infancy. The whole experience was quite enjoyable, and we had a lot of help along the way. About half of the family was female, and they assisted Letty in all of her tasks.

The boys, meanwhile, flew around and kept our cities and towns safe from crime. I had a hard time keeping track of them. They flew to all parts of the world, and this made me proud and happy. This kept the world happy as well. I would have wanted to have joined them, but my place was now by Letty's side. This included taking care of Edison, and it was a job I relished. He was getting to that age where I could begin teaching him something about flying.

So I regularly began taking him on flying excursions around the city. We were living in Los Angeles at this time, and although it did not have the cultural charm of New York, it was a large city that needed someone to look out for it. I made sure Edison and I kept out of any violent scrapes, and left the crime fighting to the police. Edison and I would call in certain situations we observed from above to the police, and went on our merry way. After all, Edison was not really old enough to learn about fighting crime. He was old enough to enjoy flying through the warm air in his father's arms.

We went out almost every day. I held Edison in my arms and we flew all over the city. When it began to get hot, I flew him out to the beach in Santa Monica and he enjoyed splashing in the cool ocean water.

"We go up in air," he would begin to say to me on a number of occasions. He was beginning to speak, and not surprisingly, a lot of what he had to say concerned flying in the air.

"Yes, you and I will go flying, Eddie, my boy," I would tell him.

I don't know if he understood everything, but he would smile and clap his hands at my remarks. It seemed as if he enjoyed flying as much as I did. Well, that was quite all right with me.

The real question remained when would I help to make him fly. This was not an easy question to answer. Edison was still very young and I was still afraid that giving him the power to fly at too early an age could lead to disaster of some kind. Letty agreed wholeheartedly with me.

Because of these reservations, we decided we would hold off allowing him to fly as long as possible. I would, however, continue holding him in my arms and flying him to fun and favorable destinations.

It was on one of these flying trips that something surprising happened that would change our family forever. I was flying Edison to the beach, a beach I knew of on the Pacific coast, when we suddenly hit some turbulence. I usually compensate for such an occurrence by flying lower to the ground. But when I tried it that fateful day, Edison slipped from my grasp and began falling through the air.

"My God!" I screamed, diving down to try to catch him in my arms.

Edison, however, kept falling. If I didn't catch him soon, he would fall faster and faster to his death. I was getting ready to extend my arms again and attempt once more to recover him when he began flying up through the air by himself!

It was truly unbelievable! He was only a few months old, and was flying by himself through the warm air currents.

"Papa," he gurgled as he flew by me into the sky.

I hurried after him, and finally caught him as he floated up towards some clouds. Well, now I knew the gene injections could be passed down through generations. Edison would never need an injection of any kind during the course of his life.

"Papa," he said once again as I held onto him.

I let Edison fly on his own a few times that day. Each time, I made sure I was in control of the situation. It's hard to know what a little baby will do when it finds it has the power to fly through the heavens. That old story of Icarus comes to mind.

Anyway, the question of when I would teach Edison to fly was answered. In the end, he was going to fly whether I taught him or not. The whole thing was already a part of him.

48

We're talking with Doc Bird and his fantastic flying clan—

So every member of your family can fly? Isn't that right?

DOC BIRD: Yes, that's correct, Jim. The whole family can fly, even the baby.

INTERVIEWER: And how is the baby?

DOC BIRD: Coming along rather nicely, Jim. He eats everything in sight and does a good job of keeping us busy all the time. Say hello to everyone, Edison.

EDISON: Hewoa, erweone.

DOC BIRD: He's only a few months old, Jim. Very intelligent for his age, wouldn't you say?

INTERVIEWER: Definitely, Doc. Is he going to be a member of your crime-fighting team?

JETLET: No, Jim, he's only a little boy.

DOC BIRD: He's not going to be saving anyone for some time, Jim. But I do take him on flying excursions through the city.

INTERVIEWER: Yes, very interesting. And have you stopped anyone from committing any crimes during those excursions?

DOC BIRD: No, whatever we see, we report immediately to the police.

INTERVIEWER: Great, Doc, and how about reporting to us about your wife, Letty's, condition?

DOC BIRD: Well, we wanted it to be a surprise, but, yes, Letty is pregnant again.

JETLET: Am I showing?

DOC BIRD: Yes, my dear, and I'm telling.

JANE: We had show and tell in kindergarten.

JIMMY: Jane is the only one who played.

ISAAC: Was anybody interested?

JIMMY: Only the boys, Izzy, only some of the boys.

DOC BIRD: Yes, well, now children you stop that. Nobody's interested in what Jane is showing.

JIMMY: That's what I told the boys.

INTERVIEWER: You've got a very funny family, Doc.

DOC BIRD: Yes, it keeps us going when something happens.

JIMMY: You're aware shit happens.

DOC BIRD: Jimmy, my boy, now you've done it. We're soon going to be off the air.

JIMMY: They could beep it.

JANE: I wish they would beep you.

49

I rushed Letty to the hospital while we were waiting to tape another show. She had her baby very soon thereafter. It was a little girl with light hair and a charming smile and we decided to name her, Penelope.

Letty was very happy and I was overjoyed. Little Penny was everything we hoped for. First of all, Letty and I wanted a girl of our own after taking care of so many adopted girls from around the world. Secondly, little Penny really generated some excitement into our lives. We were becoming bored with the sameness of our lives, the repetition of doing shows, and the need to help people and our planet. Little Penny made us forget everything for a while and concentrate on only her. It was just what we needed.

I couldn't help wondering if little Penny could fly on her own. I was interested if she could fly at birth, but testing this theory was out of the question. Letty wouldn't let me do it, and I really didn't want to try it on my own. What if she couldn't fly at birth? Maybe the genetic serum took a few years to kick in before the individual could fly on his or her own. I really didn't know, but I decided I would wait to find out. I was confident if little Penny could fly, she would demonstrate this ability to us in very short time. In the meantime, I really didn't want to do anything that may harm Penny in any way. She would be the one to decide when it was time to tell everyone what she could or couldn't do. Waiting was quite all right with me, after all.

Anyway, our family had swelled to 177, and so, when Penny was born Letty had all the help she would need from the many girls and boys we had adopted. There wasn't really very much for me to do. Whenever I wanted to help out, someone from the family would tell me they would take care of it and that I shouldn't worry.

After a while, I no longer worried about anything. I no longer cared. I was so bored I decided to go out and let the others help Letty with Edison and the baby. I felt ashamed and selfish with this attitude, but it was the only thing to do under the circumstances. My children, my biological offspring, were growing up without me.

50

Has Doc Bird Found a New Pal?

Doc Bird, the head of the Fantastic Flying Clan, has been seen around town with a new face.

Insiders say Tim Marar has been very friendly with the Fantastic Flying Man and they have been flying together in the skies over Los Angeles.

There's been no comment from Doc Bird, who is married to JetLet and has a family of about 180. The family currently has their own show.

No word from anyone in the family.

Meanwhile, Doc Bird has been seen with Tim at various nightclubs and hot spots around town.

Tim works on the Doc Bird and Letty Show as a writer and producer. He is not married and is said to be an activist in the gay community.

"Tim is very selective," said one friend. "If he is with Doc Bird then there's good reason to assume that they want to be considered a couple of some kind."

When asked if Tim was just helping out with fighting crime with Doc Tommy Hagenhurst, the friend replied, "I know they're super buddies."

Although Tim can't fly on his own, he was seen flying in Doc Bird's arms over the city.

"They're pals," one friend told us. "That's all you're going to get from me."

Are the two more than just friends? "They're pretty close, that's all I can say right now," said one insider. "If they are now a couple, it's going to come as quite a surprise to his wife and mega-family."

Bob Roberts reporting—

Vote In Our Poll

Would you be upset if Doc Bird was having a gay affair?

No 76 percent

Yes 16 percent

Not Sure 8 percent

51

I discovered I couldn't stop my thing from doing whatever it wanted. I had met Tim in a bar one night, and before I knew it, we had become very close. I had known Tim from the television show, and so, I was very honest with him. I told him I was seeking new challenges and new experiences and he immediately smiled and said, "I think I can help you out if you decide to trust me."

Well, Tim was one of the big shots running the television show, and therefore, I did trust him. He told me there were many experiences I still didn't know about and I wondered what these could be. Then Tim smiled and kissed me on the lips. I was shocked. I never thought of making love to a man before. No, I guess I did fantasize about it many times while growing up, but it always seemed so frowned upon by the society I was living in. Tim changed all that.

I used to make fun of those in the gay community. I was like many others who really didn't understand the close relationships and compassion that many felt in that so-called alternate lifestyle. Although I had spoken to a few gay people through my life and always found them somewhat pleasurable, I never took the time to really get to know any of them.

Tim made me see that I had been wrong. After kissing me and telling me there were experiences he wanted me to take part in, I made love to Tim at his house in Santa Monica.

Everything had changed forever. I was now in love with Tim, although I was still afraid to tell anyone about it. I still feared the prejudice and persecution associated with being gay and knew Letty might not understand. I realized what I had done to Letty, although we had built a huge family to help us in our times of need.

Tim was active in the gay community and he told me all about how people hated anyone with a different point of view or style of life. Things were slowly changing from the days when a gay person would get beat up on the streets or ridiculed endlessly for choosing to love a member of the same gender. Many had been killed, and Hitler had assigned them to the death camps in Germany, just as he had with the Jewish people and gypsies.

I felt a little odd about being gay myself, and then decided it really didn't matter in a world of war and violence. Wasn't it better to make love to someone, no matter what gender they were, than to want to kill or injure them? To me, the answer was quite obvious.

Besides, I was getting sick of making love to women. Letty was nice and so was the life we had made, except I found women to be rather vain and superficial. The lovemaking had become repetitious and I found men to be a new and exciting challenge. They were, of course, more aggressive than women, but this boldness is also what made men more successful and talented than most women. The lovemaking was, of course, very physical and very satisfying. I was worried about doing some of the things Tim wanted me to do, but I decided to do them anyway.

Tim liked to get high while performing sex, and so, I did the same. We experimented with cocaine, speed, and pot, and had some of the most pleasant experiences one could ask for. While on speed, I felt as though I were really a superman, and could run around the world if I wanted to. The world was only 24,000 miles around I told myself and this was really not much distance to cover while running.

Those days with Tim were some of the most enjoyable I ever spent, although I don't remember much of it. We were stoned most of the time, and made love in hundreds of ways. I lost count after a while, all the moves and positions Tim introduced me to being quite pleasurable, especially when stoned. I really wanted to tell Letty and maybe invite her to share some of the sex with the two of us, but decided she had more important things to do raising Edison and Penny.

I thought about what would happen when people found out what Tim and I were doing. Then I decided I really didn't care any longer. It was all this celebrity superstar thing that had gotten me in this situation in the first place. People wanted their superstars to stay clean and impart to them the wisdom of the ages, but most celebrities were not up to it. I mean look at all the temptations in a superstar's life. They were better looking than most people, not smarter, and so, sex was easy to obtain, as well as any drug they wanted. If you wanted wisdom, people would have to seek out the Nobel Prize winners, although I doubted any of them really knew the secrets of life and living.

No, most people were just looking for some entertainment for their spare dollars, and that's really all a superstar was expected to provide. Most of them would be forgotten in time. That's what I soon realized as I lived longer: most of these superstars never really lasted until they died. Most usually faded and then surfaced again when it was their time to go — to eternity. There was an obit, one realized how fast time went for everybody, and then they were gone. It was nothing really important in the scheme of things. They were just people whose names were known by everybody. Thinking of something they did or said, a line or a joke, was usually impossible. They had entertained during their time among the lights, and that was all that was important.

52

DOC BIRD MAKING AN ARMY OF FLYING GAY MEN?

Doc Bird, the Fantastic Flying Man, is trying to create an army of flying gay men, friends and family are charging.

That's right, some who know Doctor Tommy Hagenhurst say that he intends to build an army of flying gay men as revenge against females and family.

"He's already allowed several gay men to fly," says one insider. "He wants hundreds to fly before the end of the year."

Doc Hagenhurst is still married to Letty or JetLet and has a family of about 180 adopted children. He has two children, a boy and a girl, with Letty.

"He got sick of the whole female and family thing," says one friend. "He was looking for adventure and found it in the gay community."

Doc Bird has had a history of sex, drugs, and fame. He reputedly had affairs with about 150 women while married to the actress Tao Dade. He then married Letty Holden and began a family of adopted children that swelled to about 180, including two of his own children.

Friends say Letty is furious with Doc Bird over his gay affairs and has threatened not to let him see his children. Meanwhile, the Doc Bird and JetLet Show has been canceled by the network.

Doc Bird's alleged lover, Tim Marar, happens to be a writer and producer for that same show.

"Tim has more influence over Doc Bird than anyone," says one insider. "He wanted Doc Hagenhurst to experience an alternate lifestyle."

Doc Bird has allegedly had affairs with as many as 25 men. After he makes love to them, he helps them to fly through the air.

"Stop him before we have an army of flying faggots filling the skies," said one associate. "He doesn't know what the hell he is doing."

Many disagree.

"Oh, he knows what he's doing all right," said one friend. "He wants to live a life of adventure and this is the way he is doing it."

Will it be an army?

"If that's what he wants to do, who can stop him?" asked one insider.

His wife and their female children are the only females that can fly at this present date.

"He has nothing against females," says one friend. "He might even want to help lesbians to fly."

So far, there's no word from Doc Bird.

It is said he is planning to do a realty television show with Marar in the near future.

"It's going to be about flying with different kinds of people," said one person familiar with the project. "He'll be flying with gays, straights and everyone in between."

How about with members of his own family? "That's to be decided at a later date," says one insider. "First, he wants to get the show on the air."

How many will be in the air at that time is still not known.

-END-

53

We're here with Doctor Tommy, y'all, he's the Fantastic Flying Man—
Doc Bird, everybody!
(Applause)
Let's bring him out, it's Doc Bird, everybody!
(Applause)
You're looking pretty good, doctor, is there any reason for that?
DOC BIRD: Well, I've changed my lifestyle just a little bit, Opal.
(Laughter)
Are you coming out, Doc Bird, right here on this show?
DOC BIRD: Yes, Opal, I'm here to say I'm gay and very happy.
Doc Bird, y'all!
(Applause)
And how many affairs have you had?
DOC BIRD: I would say about 60, Opal.
And what about JetLet, Doc Bird?
DOC BIRD: Letty has a lot of help with all the children we adopted, Opal. I didn't know I was going to fall in love with men, believe me. Do you think anyone would do that if they had a choice? It all goes back to childhood when our sexuality is first developing.
When did you first think about men as being lovers?
As a young kid growing up in a harsh environment. Although my parents stayed together, they fought all the time, Opal. My best friends were males who I hung around with.
Did you have any sexual encounters at an early age?
I was really still interested in girls at a young age, Opal. But there were times when boys figured in my life as potential lovers. One male friend

got undressed in front of me and made me very excited. There were a few examples of this throughout my life.

Were you gay when you married Tao and Letty?

Yes, I guess so. I mean I was interested in females, and have had a real love for them all my life, but men provided a new excitement, new adventures I had never experienced before.

Are you helping all these men to fly after you make love to them?

Yes, that seems to be what has happened. I usually make love to them and then I help them to fly. I don't know why I'm creating all these flying people, but I did want everyone in the human race to fly at one time.

Has that changed, doc?

No, not really, although I'm waiting for the right time to announce the secret to everyone. When that time will come, I don't know any longer.

We're talking to Doc Bird, everybody!

54

AMERICAN HERO

These twelve people have been chosen as possible associates of the Fantastic Flying Man, Doctor Tommy Hagenhurst. Now they will live together, work together, and reveal hidden secrets to one another under the watchful eyes of Doc Bird. The one left standing will be given the power of flight and a chance to live a life as a genuine American Hero...

DOC BIRD: There are no jokes or songs this time around. This time I'm looking for someone who will be my associate and help me battle crime throughout the world. It doesn't matter if this person is a male or a female. All that matters is that they are qualified for the position. This is no walk in the park. It's a hard job with loving and living combined with a caring for the human race. Anyone not fit for the job will be asked to leave. Walk away. The winner will fly with me to unknown destinations for the adventure of their lives. The world will welcome the new American Hero—

This is Lonnie, she is strong and healthy and very much wants to fly. I can help her dream come true if I choose...

This is Hubert, a powerful man whose only wish is to help people. He had a hard time growing up and I can make his life easy if I choose...

This is Austin, a good-looking man who wants to fly. He wants to take care of the human race and I can take care of what he wants if I choose...

This is Dennis, a strong and powerful man who likes people and wants to help the planet. He may be the hero we've been searching for and I can make it all happen if I choose...

This is Shika, a good and kind woman who wants to fly and help the human race. I can help her achieve her greatest aspirations if I choose...

There are also Cade and Wendy and Rudy and Sani and Kito and Trish and Lathan, all of whom dream of a better world and a chance to fly through the heavens and save the planet below. I can help all of their dreams come true, but only if I choose...

This is American Hero—

The first step in becoming the American Hero is caring about our fellow human beings. I will divide our heroes into two groups and then send them off with some police officers to find out what it takes to become a true American hero. The officers will assign the contestants to various tasks that will help reveal which of these hopefuls has what it takes. In the coming weeks, we will be finding out quite a lot about each of our possible heroes. In the end, I will choose one of them to help fly with me in a chance to save innocent people and help the planet...

This first task will take everything they know about self-defense and survival. But first I must divide them in two equal teams. The police officers will help with each of the tasks—

Tonight is only the first step in revealing the American Hero. Stay with us—

55

I was back on top, although it was quite different this time around. I no longer spoke to Letty or the children. I tried several times, but Letty told me her family wasn't interested in being with me anymore. She said I had betrayed their trust and something like that could never be repaired.

"You go with your men," Letty told me. "My family doesn't want anything to do with you anymore."

"But what about Edison and little Penny," I argued. "I would like to see them one of these days."

"They're ashamed of you, Tommy," she warned. "The other children where they go to school have said some things about you."

"But I want to see them, need to see them."

"Nothing we can do about that, Tommy," she replied. "I think it's better for them if you had nothing to do with them. Eddie was particularly upset hearing about what you were doing."

"But I can explain everything—"

"It's past explaining, Tommy. You made your decision when you decided to be with all those men. Now no one in this family wants to be with you, Tommy. Can't you understand?"

That's the last time I spoke to Letty. I never did see Edison or Penny. As I was walking away from the house, Isaac called to me.

"You blew it big time, flying man," he shouted. "You upset everyone real bad."

I realized for the first time what damage I had done to my family. "I didn't mean for it to happen, Iz," I said.

"But it happened," he replied.

"Yes, it did."

"Then I don't want you to be my father anymore."

I wanted to cry upon hearing the words, but steadied myself. "That's a pretty harsh thing to say," I finally told him.

"It was meant to be," he said, running down the sidewalk and then flying into the air.

I watched him fly away and decided there was nothing I could do to convince any of them of my good intentions. I had made a selfish decision to satisfy my most inner pleasures and now I would pay the price for the rest of my life. I had tears in my eyes as I flew into the sky and away from the home Letty and I had built together.

My decision to leave them may have been a selfish one, but it was one that added to my own enjoyment of a life that had become boring and repetitious.

56

This just in—

A man who many believe is the famous Doc Bird was seen flying in a red dress over the city last night holding hands with four muscular men.

Doc Bird, who is really Doctor Tommy Hagenhurst, is said to be having gay affairs since leaving his wife, Letty, and their estimated 180 children.

"Who's going to save him?" asked one person who didn't want to be identified. "He's really gone off the deep end."

Doc Bird currently has his own reality television show entitled, "American Hero," in which one of twelve contestants is selected to be a crime-fighting hero.

There was no comment from the show's producer, Tim Marar, or from Doc Bird himself.

The man in the red dress was seen flying through the skies of the city last night at about 8 holding hands with the four men. Eyewitnesses said they were smiling and waving to everyone down below.

Doc Bird is the only one on the planet who knows how to fly without any mechanical assistance. The secret of his flight was going to be passed on to the human race, although now some people say Doc Bird has no intention of passing on that incredible secret.

Meanwhile, many friends say they are shocked and saddened by Doc Bird's recent behavior.

"He still has some responsibility for a large family," said one friend. "I don't think he should take that lightly."

-END-

57

Doc Bird, the Fantastic Flying Man, was rushed to the hospital this morning after complaining about his stomach.

The flying Doctor Tommy Hagenhurst was seen last night flying over the city in a red dress with four muscular men. There have been reports that the flying doctor has engaged in as many as 75 affairs with other gay men and that he is heavily into drugs such as speed and cocaine.

No word from Doc Bird's wife, Letty, and their 180 children, all but two of them adopted from various countries around the world.

"He was feeling ill this morning so we called 911," said one friend. "He was complaining of indigestion and an upset stomach."

Doc Bird is currently hosting a reality television series in which one of the contestants will be selected to be an American hero. No word from the producer and longtime friend, Tim Marar, on the status of the popular television program.

Doc Bird's previous television show, the Doc Bird and JetLet Show, was canceled after reports of Doc Bird having affairs with numerous gay men. He reportedly taught the men how to fly after each of the affairs.

The latest incident involving gay men resulted in Doc Bird being seen flying over the city in a red dress.

"I hope he doesn't have AIDS," said one insider. "These things happen if one is not careful and decides to do whatever he wants in order to gain a little freedom and happiness."

-END-

58

There was no doubt about it, I was dying. All the years of enjoying myself, letting my thing lead me in the quest for new experiences, had finally caught up to me. Now there was nothing left for me to do except bow out gracefully. I was still a superstar in the eyes of many, but little good that would do me in battling a death sentence. The real worth of stardom was very little after the lights had dimmed and the money was no longer flowing into a bank account.

I thought of Letty and the children and wondered if any of them would visit me in the hospital. I wanted to talk with Letty again, tell her she had been right and that what I had done was really not worth it in the overall scheme of things. I wondered if any of the children, especially Eddie and Penny, would ever talk to me again knowing all the sordid things I had done.

I knew I was a hopeless case, but one day decided to fight back. I would stop having gay affairs and take my life back. The men I had met really never did anything to improve my life and so I felt I really didn't owe them anything in deciding my future. I now had plenty of time to read and reflect on life and decided maybe I should begin reading the Bible.

There were certain people who visited me in the hospital who convinced me that the Bible had many teachings about sin and redemption, and that this path could lead me to a renewed life on the planet. I thought about it and decided they might be right.

There was no doubt that I was a sinner. Yes, a sinner and that believing in God and the Bible could help me overcome these sins of mine. I would also do charity work and try to help people living on the planet. Yes, I knew many people had already condemned me to hell, but there was still time to change that path, still time to be born again.

The first thing you have to do to be born again is to think positively. Yes, I began seeing everything in a positive manner, and decided anything negative could be turned into a positive. Transform a negative to a positive is what the church people taught me. It all had something to do with seeing the light, the light of spirituality and the light of an all-powerful God.

I was told I could rid myself of all sin by accepting the Savior and letting him into my life. After all, He had died on the cross for my sins, and therefore, I was devoid of all sin if I let him into my life. In this way, I was going to shed myself of all previous sins and become totally born again in the eyes of the Lord. Anyone who didn't believe or couldn't believe or were just born into another religion were to be despised. There was only one true religion and only one true path to God. Jews, Muslims, Buddhists, Hindus and all others were bound for hell where they would burn for eternity. I would live in heavenly bliss, adored by heaven, and welcomed into its midst when my earthly life was over. I would be renewed and without sin and would therefore be one of the Lord's chosen.

It obviously was the right thing for me to do. There was nothing for me to lose, and yet, I could gain so much. The choice was an easy one. I now had the chance to be sinless and to accuse everybody else of being unworthy heretics and heathens. They would not be forgiven by the Lord unless they listened to what I told them. Yes, an easy choice to make.

59

This is American Hero, Giving to One and All—

Welcome everybody, this is Doc Bird. Today we will be giving back to all those people out there who need our assistance. You, our faithful audience, is as much a part of this show as any of us. Please feel free to use one of the numbers below to make your very needed donation to the causes we will talk about on today's show. But first, a song:

Now is the time for us to be bolder
Everything fine and all war is over
Now is the time.

Somebody said it's all right,
Somebody said we've got to keep trying.

Now is the time for you to stop fighting
God has a plan of thunder and lightning
Now is the time.

It's a time for us to think about
The way that things are going,
It's a time for us to think about
The way that time is flowing.

Now is the time.

Now is the time for us to want better
Love is the way so go out and get her
Now is the time.

Somebody said it's all right,
Somebody said, we've gotta keep trying,

Now is the time for you to stop fighting,
God has a plan of thunder and lightning,
Now is the time.

It's a time for us to think about
The way that time is going,
It's a time for us to think about
The way that time is flowing,
Now is the time.

Now is the time to want peace about here
Everything fine and all war remains fear
Now is the time.

Now is the time.

Thank you very much and stay with us—
The people of Nigeria are just like us, so why don't we see it that way. We have to make it our responsibility to give to them until all poverty and illness is gone. Won't you help us? Give as much as you can and watch as your money makes a difference—

There are so many people we can help around the world. But first stick around for Velvet Throne and Ikita as they take the stage to entertain you as American Hero gives to one and all—

60

Edison, my beloved little son, was dead. The story of how it happened is not a pleasant one for I am the one to blame. I didn't think about how my life style would affect my children and this was truly a selfish shortcoming on my part. I only realize that now as my little son is gone forever and so is a piece of my grieving heart. Ah, how foolish we are in pursuing our dreams. How fragile life really is regardless of one's personal situation.

It all happened a few days ago when I decided to visit the children at my former house. I didn't care that Letty had told me to stay away. I had a big part in putting together that family and I would not be denied seeing how they were doing even if they didn't want to see me.

Well, anyway, as I was swooping down from the sky, I noticed little Eddie playing ball in the front yard. I landed right near him and greeted him with a huge smile. He looked at me and frowned. I thought Letty had told him some things about me that she really shouldn't have and now the young boy of about 4 had grown to hate me.

"I'm your father," I said to him.

He frowned once again. "Yes, I know that," he replied.

I tried to hug him, but he twisted his body, and escaped from my arms.

"But Eddie," I said. "I wanted to tell you that I love you very much."

He frowned at me, uttered a noise of some kind, and then flew off into the sky. I could do nothing but follow.

Eddie was born ready to fly. It was in his DNA. I know because I'm the one responsible. Because Eddie could fly naturally at birth, it was rather hard to follow him. He had already become somewhat of an expert flyer.

He zipped above the trees and buildings, swooped down towards the ground, and then rocketed back into the sky. I tried following his every move, but he was just too quick.

"Eddie, you don't understand!" I began shouting to him. "I didn't do anything to hurt you!"

But nothing I said could stop him from flying into the distance. Finally, he began slowing down seemingly waiting for me to catch up. As I got closer, however, he turned and frowned with tears in his eyes.

"I don't want to live anymore," he shouted back at me. "Do you understand?"

Before I could answer him, Eddie took off like a bullet into the blue sky. I watched him as he raced off in a straight line towards the sun. He was like a rocket headed for the perils of outer space and there was not one thing I could really do about it. Eddie was soon gone forever.

"No, no," I muttered to myself in my despair. "It can't be happening, no, no, Eddie."

I tried looking for him, but found nothing when I soared above the clouds. Eddie was gone.

I decided I would go back and tell Letty, and then try to come to terms with what happened. I knew it was something I would never get over, but I resolved I would try. Try to begin again if it was at all possible. Eddie took with him all of my joy and hope for the future, and now I would have to find a new reason to live. I knew it wouldn't be easy, but there really wasn't any alternative. I would do it for Eddie, whether he wanted it that way or not. Yes, for Eddie, my beloved little son.

61

This just in—

Doc Bird, whose real name is Doctor Tommy Hagenhurst, has announced his candidacy for the U.S. Senate. Doc Bird, who is capable of flying without any mechanical assistance, has assured the public that he is prepared to reveal the secret of unaided flight at a later time.

His rivals for the Senate seat have complained that Doc Bird is using his gift of flight to quote "bribe the people of this state to vote for him."

Doc Bird, who says he has recently become a born again, will run as a Conservative. Once known for his slogan, Peace is Half a Fist, the flying doctor now says he'll run under the slogan, More War, Choose Life.

Doc Bird has claimed to have turned his life completely around, having once been accused of extramarital affairs with men and women. How he will explain all these past occurrences will be key to whether he is successful in seeking the Senate seat.

Meanwhile, his wife, Letty, has apparently agreed to campaign for him. The two were said to be headed for divorce, having already adopted about 180 children.

Now Doc Bird says those children will help him in his election bid.

"We will be flying all through the state to convince the voters I am the right man for the job," he told people gathered at a rally. "We will be telling people to vote for more war, life, and an end to environmental obstacles."

In other news—

62

Why do you liberals hate this country? That's what I'm talking about. They don't support our war efforts and want more government in our lives. Kill, baby, kill, that's what I'm saying. Anyone who doesn't support this country should be killed, yes, killed. More war, that's what we're saying. More war and choose life. No abortions and the death penalty. More war and choose life. Life until we choose to take it away in a war or by lethal injection. Yes, we can do it. We need change in this country, change that means the government is out of our lives and the rich don't get penalized. What's wrong with that? And no environmental obstacles. Drill, baby, drill until the stuff comes spilling out onto our beaches. That's what I say. We need our energy independence, no matter the cost of doing business. You want pristine beaches and thriving sea life, go to a South Pacific island. Here we take care of our people. I'm not worried about these endangered animals pointed out by the liberal environmentalists. Kill, baby, kill. If they want to live, let them find another habitat. Why do we need these moronic animals, anyway? Does it really matter if the tiger goes extinct? Who the hell cares? Why do we need a tiger on this planet, anyway? Kill, baby, kill. That's what I'm saying. More war, choose life, and support the death penalty. I'm Doc Bird and that's what I stand for in this upcoming election. I love my country and will not let these leftist fags give it back to the Indians. Understand? Everybody has a right to own a gun and, by God, I'll see to it that everyone has a gun in their possession if I'm elected. I need your vote to make my visions a reality. Vote for Doc Bird for Senator. Thank you and good luck—

63

DOC BIRD: You leftist fag, you would give our country away to the fags, Communists and illegals.

BILL McCALL: Why, you're nothing but a fascist pig, Hagenhurst.

DOC BIRD: You tell that to all the good Americans out there who believe in good old American values—

BILL McCALL: And what are those values? To hate everyone who is not like you?

DOC BIRD: No, I'm not telling anyone to hate anyone. I'm just saying that there are people who still love this country and everything it stands for and wouldn't mind holding a gun and fighting for what's rightfully theirs. That's all I'm saying. This country belongs to the good people who believe in war and dying for freedom and country. This country belongs to the good people who believe it's wrong taking a life from the womb. This country belongs to the good people who believe it's wrong to take a life and anyone who does will have to forfeit a life. This country belongs to the good people who believe it's their right to bear arms and will blow anyone away who decides to take away their natural-born rights. That's what I'm saying. Give America back to Americans—

BILL McCALL: A woman should have the right to have a say in her own pregnancy, Tommy. You're only defending the rich, as I see it. Let all men and women live equally in society—

DOC BIRD: I'm talking about giving the country back to real Americans. Americans who want to pass their family values on and see this country fulfill its destiny as the greatest country in the history of the world.

BILL McCALL: Hey, Tommy, wasn't your father a black doctor? Who are the real Americans, anyway? This country was built on its immigrants, people who migrated from other countries. You're nothing but a fraud, doctor. You're just pandering to conservative Americans. I want to work for all Americans throughout this entire great country. Who is Doctor Tommy Hagenhurst, anyway? Is it the one who fooled around with all those women behind his wife's back? Is it the one who fooled around with all those men behind his wife's back? Seems to me Doctor Tommy Hagenhurst is nothing but a philandering fraud, that's the way I see it—

DOC BIRD: That's the way you see it, Bill, because you're a myopic Communist. Everyone knows what I have done through my life and everyone knows I have paid back to society by helping people. I also assure you that everyone will learn to fly if I'm elected. That secret will soon be revealed and then this society will truly change for the better. I know what it is to be taken in by the liberal media and then shot in the back by those who professed to care about you. All of these so-called superstars running around who think they can do anything that pleases them for the moment. But there is a price to pay. Yes, a price and I know that better than anyone. And now that I've learned those lessons, I'm here to tell you that this country can be great again if we just stop listening to the liberal media and give this country back to its real Americans, all Americans who believe in freedom and democracy—

BILL McCALL: There he goes again. The doctor fraud is trying to be a demagogue for the right side of America. We're all real Americans, doctor, for your information. And every one of us came from somewhere else, except for the Native Americans. And we all believe in freedom and democracy, we're just not going to get it by destroying Americans who don't believe the same way we do—

DOC BIRD: My opponent fails to understand that there are opposing forces who wish to dictate how we are born, how we die and everything in between. I'm saying that it should be our decision, not some lawmaker's. Taking a life from the womb of a mother goes against natural laws. My opponent will disagree. Going to war is necessary to defend freedom and democracy throughout the world. My opponent will disagree. There should be a gun in everyone's hands and they have a right to use it when their natural rights are violated. My opponent will disagree. These are some of the things we disagree about. I say we should defend the future so we can go soaring through it into a new age of freedom. Yes, my friends, I will take you into a new age of freedom. An age of freedom and flight.

BILL McCALL: My opponent is trying to bribe the people of this state into voting for a philandering fraud. He tries to influence the people by continually promising to make us all fly. Well, all right, doctor, why don't you do it now?

DOC BIRD: My opponent is impatient about some things and willing to wait forever on more important matters. The time will come when everyone is free and flying, but right now we have to help our country. We have to help it if we truly love it.

BILL McCALL: I love this country better than you, Tommy. We all love this country better than you. You're the one who took those women in the air and made love to them on American landmarks. Is that love for our country? To make love on George Washington's head? Is that love for one's country? This is the person who showed disdain for all things American and free by making love on the Kremlin!

DOC BIRD: The Russians happen to be valuable allies, Bill. And most of that stuff they say I did was just rumor and innuendo. Most of it was as untrue as your allegations. If I did it on American landmarks, it was out of love for those landmarks and my American heritage.

BILL McCALL: You don't love your country! Bill McCall loves this country! Bill McCall will show all Americans what it is to be an American by leading by example. We don't need to fly through the trees like some stupid bird brains. Leave that to the scientists who have nothing better to do. Leave that to the scientists who just want another way to satisfy their perverse libidos. This guy is nothing but a fraud, ladies and gentlemen. He will lead you into the abyss. He wants all of you to fly, but if you elect him, you will all fall into the pit of darkness. Listen to me, ladies and gentlemen, before it's too late.

DOC BIRD: Right, Bill, we're all going land in the land below if we don't elect you. What a bunch of hogwash. I've already changed my life from one of sin and indulgence to one of spirituality and righteousness. It wasn't easy. No, not easy at all. But if I'm elected, I'll help everyone rid themselves of sin and corruption and become satisfied members of the Lord's realm. Yes, that's right, people, let Doc Bird teach you how to do it right.

BILL McCALL: You've got to be kidding, doc. You're going to teach us how to do it right? You? The same guy who goes cavorting around with men and women while lawfully married with hundreds of adopted children and his own children? This is the guy who is going to teach us how to be free?

Ridiculous. Why this man is nothing more than a toxic person looking to infect the general population. Toxic, I say. That's the kind of person this doctor is. He's full of sin whether he says he's born again or not. I don't trust him and I don't think you should either. Toxic, that's what I say.

DOC BIRD: The only thing that's toxic, Bill, is your after shave lotion. You would know about toxic, though, because under your administration more toxic waste has been found dumped along our waterways than ever before. It's the same old thing if you elect Bill McCall. The same old government butting into our lives, the same old politician looking for a way to tax the good people of this state until they can figure out a way to balance the budget. Well, I've had enough people, and I know you have, too. I've had enough of politicians attacking each other about their own shortcomings. I've had enough of the government looking into our lives. It's time for a change and Doctor Tommy Hagenhurst is that change. Let's not waste our votes on the same old thing, vote for Doctor Tommy Hagenhurst and a time for change. Thank you.

We're out of time. That concludes today's debate between Doctor Tommy Hagenhurst and Bill McCall, candidates for the United States Senate...

64

Doctor Tommy Hagenhurst formally rid himself of all sin and indulgence in a ceremony down by the water. (*Video footage shows Doc Bird being baptized by the Born Agains*) His opponent, Bill McCall, formally surrendered to special interests and tax lovers by failing to balance the budget. (*Video footage of Bill McCall's locked office*) Is this the kind of man you want to lead you into the great unknown? Doctor Tommy Hagenhurst has dedicated his life to helping people no matter who they were. His record of saving people speaks for itself. Doc Bird is known throughout the country and now he wants to help this state against the special interests and the tax lovers. (*Video showing Doc Bird smiling, shaking hands, and then flying into the air*) Won't you help him? Vote Doctor Tommy Hagenhurst for U.S. Senate. *I'm Doc Bird and I wholeheartedly endorse this message.* Doctor Tommy Hagenhurst for Senate.

65

I was back on top once again. Now I had a new purpose defining my life, a new reason to pick my head up in the morning. I was on my way to becoming a United States Senator. At least, that's what the polls said. Yes, according to the polls, I was leading my opponents by as much as 15 percent. My publicity people told me if I didn't make any major mistakes, I would probably win. I couldn't believe it. After all I had been through, I was heading towards respectability.

The only thing left to do was to patch things up with Letty. I had been wrong in seeking out new experiences and finding myself making love to all those men. I belonged with Letty and the children. I knew they really didn't need me anymore, but I decided they probably could use my experience to find the answer to living a good life. I had something to offer them, something to make their lives a little better.

I was still distraught over Edison. There was so much I wanted to tell him and show him, and now he was gone. It just wasn't right. Someone upstairs had made a mistake. Oh, well, I decided I would make my peace with God and move on.

The only question now was if Letty was willing to take me back. I know I had made many mistakes, but so had God. My place was being by Letty's side, bringing up all of those children we adopted together. And there was also Penny to raise and love. I wanted to be there with them as they went through the lessons of life. I had something to share. Something to add to their lives.

When I first tried to get in touch with Letty again, she had nothing but disdain for me. "Is this about the election, Tommy?" she asked with an angry look in her eyes.

"No, I really want to see you and the kids again," I told her. "It isn't right for them to grow up without a father."

"Some father you turned out to be, Tommy."

"You don't understand, Letty. I felt useless. Nobody needed me. What was I supposed to do?"

"You weren't supposed to go off and make love to all those men."

"But they were giving me something I wasn't getting at home, Letty. They were giving me love and affection."

"More like love and infection, Tommy."

"You don't understand, Letty, I needed them. And they needed me. They were the only ones who really needed me."

"I needed you, Tommy. But you were never around. You were off playing with all those gay men."

"But I've straightened myself out, Letty. I realize you and the children are the only ones who are really important to me."

"I think you realized that a little too late, Tommy."

"I'm asking for another chance, Letty."

"And what if I give you that other chance, Tommy."

"I'll be with you and the kids forever, darling. I'll do everything I can to make their lives better. That's what I'll do with that other chance, Letty."

She then looked at me with tears in her eyes. "Okay, Tommy," she finally said, "I'll give you another chance, but if you blow it, I'll do everything I can to destroy you any way I can. Understand? You were good to me and the children at one time, so I'm going to give you another chance and hopefully, you still remember how to live correctly."

"You're doing the right thing, Letty. I won't let you down."

I went back with Letty to the house and saw the children once again. They all said they were glad I was back and that we were one big, happy family again. They all said they wanted to give me another chance and that they were happy Letty finally agreed.

I was happy Letty had agreed. I now had a real chance of establishing a new life for myself and my family. A life as a United States Senator with all its perks and advantages. There was only one thing left to decide: would I allow everyone to fly. It was a big decision and one I didn't take lightly. I decided I would take a wait and see approach. I still wasn't sure if it was a secret I wanted the whole world to share in.

66

This is the Evening News with Russell Johnson.

Doctor Tommy Hagenhurst, also known as Doc Bird and the Flying Man, began helping people to fly today as he made his way through the state.

And according to the people he helped, Doc Bird is a better hero than Superman or Batman. Here's Bob Polter with a report.

Doc Bird fulfilled at least one promise. People were flying on the campaign trail today after the doctor injected several people with his magic flying serum.

"It's better than sex," said one happy voter who landed in front of this reporter. "He's a real genius."

And many others agreed as they flew off to God knows where. The only one left standing with his feet on the ground was Doctor Tommy Hagenhurst. He's running for the Senate, you know.

"I just felt I had a responsibility to these people who I had promised so many times in the past," said Doc Bird. "Now at least I can say I made one promise come true."

And that's very true. The only thing many people are asking now is whether Doc Bird should have kept his flying juice a secret.

"The world will never be the same again," said one bystander. "Why these people will be able to go anywhere they want."

Many already have. Two people have already contacted the local sports teams about playing for them in the upcoming season. Some have decided to dance in the skies. One person reportedly flew off to the top of Mount Everest.

"It really gives the person a feeling of unbelievable freedom," said one of the people injected by the doctor. "I mean you're no longer bound to the planet."

Meanwhile, Doc Bird continued to campaign for the U.S. Senate seat. His main opponent, Bill McCall, continued to attack Doctor Hagenhurst as a philandering fraud. Tell that to the people who are flying overhead tonight. Reporting from the campaign trail, this is Bob Polter—

67

We're talking with Buddy Blag, who was given the gift of flight by Doctor Tommy Hagenhurst, better known as Doc Bird—

INTERVIEWER: How did Doc Bird allow you to fly?

BUDDY: He gave me a shot of some kind.

INTERVIEWER: Did it hurt?

BUDDY: Not really, it hurt for a few seconds like any other shot.

INTERVIEWER: And then what happened?

BUDDY: Well, it was like my body was collapsing. I suddenly felt much lighter and more agile.

INTERVIEWER: Then you just began to fly?

BUDDY: Well, there's some practice before you can actually fly. You have to practice jumping off things and hovering in the air. Then after some practice, you just begin to fly in the air.

INTERVIEWER: Is it enjoyable?

BUDDY: Nothing like it in the world, my friend. You've never felt so free in your entire life.

INTERVIEWER: Did you go anywhere special?

BUDDY: Everywhere you go when you're flying is something or somewhere special. I mean I landed on a light pole just like a little bird. It was so amazing and I looked down and smiled thinking there's nothing in the world better than this. Nothing.

INTERVIEWER: I hear many of the people who were able to fly went to much more exotic sites?

BUDDY: Yeah, you could go anywhere in the world. I decided to go to Hawaii and then to a small island in the Pacific Ocean. I probably was the first person ever to land on the island. That's what makes Doc Bird's discovery so unbelievable. I mean I heard one of the people flew to the top of Mount Everest. Another flew over that volcano in Iceland. Nothing is really impossible once you learn to fly.

INTERVIEWER: Did you have to pay Doc Bird anything?

BUDDY: Not a dime. He's not like these money-hungry companies looking to charge you every month and for every little thing they can think of. Doc Bird is one classy guy, that's all I can say.

INTERVIEWER: Are you married, Mr. Blag?

BUDDY: Yeah, my wife can fly, too.

INTERVIEWER: Did you fool around in the air?

BUDDY: I'm not the only one, I can tell you that.

INTERVIEWER: Did you take her anywhere special?

BUDDY: We went flying over the Atlantic Ocean. It was beautiful. I mean you can really fly into the water if you have the nerve and then fly back into the sky just like a gull. We flew all the way to Spain and then turned around and came back. It was great.

INTERVIEWER: Will your children fly without the serum, Mr. Blag?

BUDDY: That's what the doc told me after he injected both of us. He said that usually the children are able to fly on their own without any assistance of any kind. I don't know if that's true. I guess we'll see what happens in the future.

We've been talking to Buddy Blag, who is able to fly due to being injected by Doc Bird. More after these messages—

68

Now it looks as if I'm going to be elected United States Senator. My main opponent, Bill McCall, made a huge mistake when he told the voters he had fought in Vietnam. The only problem was Bill McCall was nowhere near Vietnam and it turns out he was shuffling papers back in the States during the war years. The big idiot made himself to be a hero in a war he never fought in. Well, the voters were pretty angry about that and now I hear McCall is dropping in the polls. I was already ahead by at least 10 percent. Now it looks as if the election is mine if I don't screw up.

Letty has agreed to help me campaign and so have the children. It's the best news I heard and I celebrated by flying from one end of the state to the other. This is really the good news I've been waiting for. With Letty and the children helping me, I don't think any of my opponents has any real chance. The family can cover the whole state in one day. And with Bill McCall opening his big yap, there really is nothing that can stop us now.

I was so proud of Letty. She told everyone on the campaign trail that I was the best man for the state. She said I was dedicated to helping people and didn't even care if I got paid for it. Then she told everyone that flying had changed her life and that I was going to change everyone's life by teaching the world to fly.

The children were also delightful. They sang songs on the campaign trail and shook everybody's hand. Then they sang, Elect Doc Bird He's As Good As You've Heard. It was simply wonderful.

The campaign stops are packed now as I make my way across the state. It really seems as if it's my election to lose. The people are excited about someone new on the ballot and about getting the chance to fly. I am trying to make my speeches fairly short and to the point. Nobody likes to stand there and hear someone speak for a long time, it's rather boring. But after I speak, I pick a few people to be injected, and soon they're flying out into the clear, blue skies. There's nothing on earth that can really beat the feeling. Nothing.

69

Bill McCall says he's a Vietnam vet. The records show he never served anywhere near Vietnam. What else has he lied about? Doctor Tommy Hagenhurst has told the voters the whole truth and nothing but the truth. He has come clean. Why hasn't Bill McCall? If you want your U.S. Senator to be honest and true, vote for Doctor Tommy Hagenhurst. He won't try to tell you something that never happened. He'll only try to make you fly like you've never done before. Doctor Tommy Hagenhurst for U.S. Senate.

I'm Doc Bird and I approve this message—

We're speaking with Doc Bird, Doctor Tommy Hagenhurst—
Do you have any kind of war record?

Well, it wasn't a war but I've served this country by saving as many people as I could by flying through the air. My opponent has said he fought in Vietnam, which is an outright lie. He has never saved one person in a war he never fought in and he has never saved anyone during peacetime.

Are you going to continue to teach people how to fly?

Yes, I'm going to continue to speak across this state and then help people to fly.

Can you teach me?

Certainly. We can do it right now if you'd like. I've already injected this man a few weeks ago and now he is ready to fly. Do you feel lighter than before?

Yes, definitely lighter than ever.

Well, that's good. Now we'll bring out a few boxes for you to practice with.

I'm not going to break my neck or anything, will I?

Hopefully not. I just want to see you climb up two boxes and jump off. That's all.

Okay, I'm up here on two boxes. I'm now going to jump off the boxes.

How was that?

It felt very good, as if I was gliding down from a tree.

Well, this is just the first part. It takes a lot more practice before you can just go soaring off. Let's take the next step. You climb back up those two boxes and begin flapping your arms. If you like, we can give you artificial wings to use. But you see the real challenge is getting used to flying through the air.

Yes, I understand what you're saying. You have to take this one step at a time. Isn't that right?

Yes, you have to be very careful that you have the technique right before you can venture into the skies.

Let me try it once again. I'm going to climb up onto the boxes and jump off. This time, however, I'm going to try to fly a little bit.

Just remember to keep your arms stiff and moving at all times. Everything else should go smoothly.

Here I go, doc. Hey, look at me, everyone.

That wasn't too bad. You should be flying in no time at all. You've already taken the first steps in the process. You see after repeated attempts, one suddenly finds the right technique for them and then suddenly fly off into the blue skies.

I'll try it again, doc. The third time is usually the charm. I've already felt as if I was flying a little bit.

Okay, try it again. Many people have started flying on their third attempt.

Has anyone been successful on their first attempt?

My children, Keisha and Isaac, did it on their first try. But it is very rare.

Okay, here I go, doc. Let's see what happens on the third time. Hey, I'm flying, everyone.

(The interviewer flies across the set and then out through an opened door.)

I guess we'll be back after these messages—

70

I was speaking to Penny for the first time since she had grown a little bit and I asked her if she missed having a father in the house.

"Yes," she said with a cute frown. "Because Mommy is lonely and the children all want to hear stories and play with you like we did when you were here."

"But you have people to play with," I said. "You have all the other children and the nannies and Mommy."

"But it isn't the same without you," she insisted. "You know about flying better than anyone and we need to hear some things so we don't get into trouble like Edison."

"Have you ever been in trouble?" I asked.

"Yes, plenty of times," she replied. "But Mommy or Keisha or Ka-Ching or Isaac or somebody is always there to help me."

"Where do you go flying?"

"I'm not allowed to go too far. I fly around and then after a few minutes, I have to fly back with Mommy because they say I could find myself going too high or too far. Everyone is very worried about me and they say they want to take care of me and make sure nothing happens like it did to Edison. But all I really wanted was to fly with my Daddy because he knows so much about it and wouldn't let me get into any kind of trouble."

"You're right about that, Penny, darling," I told her. "I would never let anything happen to you. Your brother just didn't understand. I tried to tell him, but he didn't want to listen. But you will listen, Penny, dear, won't you?"

"Oh, yes, Daddy, I'll listen. You take me flying and I will listen to everything you say."

"That's fine, darling. Take my hand."

I went flying with Penny that day and everything seemed right with the world. We were laughing and soaring and met quite a few people flying off in other directions. I think the world will be a good place to live once again when everybody is flying on their own. Just imagine it. Nobody will ever be bounded to the planet again. Whenever one desires, one can just fly off to whatever destination he or she chooses. The planet will be one big paradise. Yes, that's what I was shooting for. The planet becoming one big paradise in which everyone knows no bounds or limits.

I took Penny back that day with a new sense of being. Everything seemed to delight me. We were on the verge of becoming totally free.

71

Click to view video—

I'm Doc Bird, the Fantastic Flying Man, and I'm helping the world to fly. Just watch me—

(Doc Bird soars through the sky)

Anybody can do it, it's really quite easy. All you have to do is get the required injection and then you are ready to take off into the skies. The only side effects of the injection seem to be delirious fun and excitement. But don't worry your whole family can join in. I know because mine is flying in the blue skies every day.

(Doc Bird is flying over the distant landscape)

This is freedom as never experienced before. Yes, once you can fly without mechanical assistance, who knows what you will be capable of doing.

(Doc Bird landing on his feet)

It's all within our reach, people. The time to make this place a paradise is at hand. I'm Doc Bird and I'm looking forward to seeing you in the clear, blue skies.

End of video—

What we really need is another war before all the people are able to make this truly a paradise.

We're talking to Doc Bird, the Fantastic Flying Man, who is running for the United States Senate—

You think war is inevitable?

Yes, I do. Every period of human history has been punctuated by war. It is the thing that holds our society together. Everyone knows there are evil forces out there who would like to take our freedoms away from us. It is these evil forces which we have been fighting since the beginning of time. It is no different now. There are still evil forces in our world who would like to tell us how to worship, how to make love, and how to govern our people. The only way to prevent these evil forces from taking over is by war. A good war. A war everybody can get behind and really rally to victory. Yes, there's nothing better than a good war. It is the way of humanity, the way of the Bible. We must eradicate these evil forces before we can truly love one another.

Then are you saying it's all right to take another's life?

Yes, the Bible tells us an eye for an eye. We must take lives to protect our own lives. Protecting our country and fighting for the right to be free is the only thing that matters in this world. We take lives all the time. The death penalty is one way and war is another. Let's just not take the life from the womb. That's the only life we really have to be concerned with. Taking a life on the battlefield or in the prison is all right if it saves other lives. Let everyone have a gun and let's shoot it out. Kill, baby, kill. That's what it's all about.

So then you're advocating another war?

It's the only thing the human race really does right. I mean war stimulates all kinds of creative and technological thoughts and leads to a booming economy. It's been responsible for so many advances through the centuries. Everyone loves to rally around a war, it gives patriotic thrills to everyone fighting or watching at home. And people really feel as if they are doing something constructive. I mean people feel as if something is being done about the evil forces in the world and that their freedom is being protected. Yes, there's nothing like fighting for freedom in the world. It really is the best thing the human race does or has ever done. Wars have really advanced civilization throughout the centuries.

So you're saying war is advantageous to the people?

Yes, there's nothing like a war to make everyone happy. Why everyone benefits. Medicine makes great advances trying to save the wounded and ideology makes great advances in the name of saving the world. You can't beat it for taking the people's minds off their boring and pointless lives. And you can always find something to argue about. There are enough obnoxious and unkind people to always find an excuse for a war and leaders can base their whole administration on the making and fighting of wars. You just can't beat it, that's all. Wars have sculpted the ages. And the great part is it really doesn't matter who wins. It takes years and years to see the real outcome of a war and usually things revert to the status quo in the end. I mean people were screaming about how the world was becoming Communist or Socialist or something and none of their fears were ever realized. The egomaniacs from the mid-twentieth century who wanted to take over the world are all gone now. People believe there is still evil in the world, however, and therefore, there's always support for another war.

So will there be another war?

Probably there will be a war. There's always a war and always has been. What would this country be without a war? I'll tell you, boring and complacent. That's why when there is no war, an administration must find one. Look at the Reagan administration, there was no war so one was created on the tiny island of Grenada. It was a ridiculous, senseless war, but it was fought like any other war. You see there always has to be a war to keep America going. Things are done during a war and the people are united behind a cause. And young men die in the name of protecting freedom and liberty. Yes, every administration needs the patriotic surge that comes with having a war. It's essential.

So killing people for no real reason doesn't get you upset?

But there is a reason. We're killing people in the name of freedom and liberty and defending our way of life. Now I'm not saying I would favor war if mothers had abortions instead of letting their babies go off to fight in a senseless war, but I will say that war does help us unite against foreign forces who would like to see our way of life destroyed. Abortions are a terrible waste of life and goes against everything we hold sacred as a nation. It is the murder of an innocent life and I will oppose it always. But war, you see, is a dignified way to die while defending your nation against those who would want to destroy it. And the death penalty is for murdering people who don't really deserve to live unless DNA samples prove they didn't commit the crime. It is the murder of a guilty life and I will favor it always.

Shouldn't sin be forgiven?

Yes, unless the sin results in murder and mayhem. Then the person or persons should be put to death. It is the only way some crimes committed can really be forgiven. We are not God, we must do what we must and wait until we are all forgiven later.

Do you think the people feel the same way?

Oh yes, as I make my way across the state, I see nothing but support for my views and opinions. The people are tired of the politics of the past. They are waiting for change, and I will bring them that change. There will be another war and there will be less government, although government will be fighting the war. There will be no abortions, but there will be a death penalty and there will be guns for all. Those are some of the changes the people are looking for in their next senator. They want to be led onto the battlefield and defeat the evil forces seeking to defeat them and they want to be led back to a time when taxes were low and science was ignorant. This I will do as senator of this great state. And, of course, everyone will fly!

Do you plan to teach the entire world to fly?

Yes, very soon the whole world will be flying. My flying injections will soon take place all over the world and everyone will be off to places they never dreamed existed. This will bring about a new age in human history. A new age in which human beings are free to do as they please and go where they want. That is what I will bring to the human race. It will be a time when everyone is free and live as they wish on the planet.

When will these injections begin?

They already have started and will continue. I have shown that human beings can be taught to fly and will continue to prove this point in the months and years ahead. The only thing that is really needed right now is the worldwide distribution of serum. Once that great task is completed, everyone will be able to take advantage of this new medical technology.

Can anyone fly?

As long as they are injected and they don't weigh too much, most people will be able to fly. You have to be as light as possible to fly, and therefore, some people will have to trim down or lose some excess weight before being able to fly through the air. That's really the only thing that can hinder one attempting to fly, excess weight. But we really believe these problems can be overcome allowing everyone to experience flight at some time.

And so we're heading into a new age?

Yes, most definitely. It will be an age in which there is more freedom than ever before. We will be able to take care of the world on our own and we will be able to help anyone in need. That's the age we will soon be living in, an age of freedom and self-reliance.

We're talking to Doc Bird, the Fantastic Flying Man—

72

DOC BIRD: We're soon going to be flying and you're the only one who will be left behind.

BILL McCALL: Flying, flying. That's the only reason people have decided to vote for you, doctor. They are tired of all the important issues that face us as citizens. They just want to go flying off with you and leave all of the problems behind. But it's not that easy. No, someone's going to have to take care of the problems. And that someone is Bill McCall.

DOC BIRD: You've got to be kidding, Bill. You're not qualified to tackle the problems we are dealing with. And not everybody will be flying off to who knows where. Some people will help solve our problems. They're not that complicated. I will find a few good men to balance the budget and make sure everyone has what they need. Then we'll go flying off to who knows where.

BILL McCALL: That's not funny, Tommy. You can't just let some unqualified people do all the work for you. You have to make sure everything is done in a timely manner. This is not a job for someone who doesn't know what he's doing. This is a job for someone with some experience.

DOC BIRD: Yeah, experience like your experience in Vietnam, Bill. Well, he was never in Vietnam and he never really successfully balanced a budget. Is that the experience you're talking about? Do you want someone who lies about his experience to come in here and foul everything up like he's done in the past? Or do you want change? Good change in which people are free again and take care of the things they need to take care of. That's what I'm offering to the voters of this state.

BILL McCALL: The kind of change you are talking about the voters are not interested in, Tommy. The change you want will make us an irresponsible and lazy society. That's the change you're talking about. I'm offering the people experience in getting things done. That's something no one can get by flying around.

DOC BIRD: Experience in failure, Bill, that's what you're offering the people of this state. And flying around is nothing to sneer at, Bill, it just might liberate the human race. All you want, Bill, is the government breathing down our necks and telling us what to do all the time. Well, people have had enough, Bill, whether you realize it or not. Enough of the same old politics of failure, enough of promising things they never intend to deliver, enough of lying to the voters about a war record that doesn't exist. The people have had enough, Bill.

BILL McCALL: They will soon have enough of flying around in circles and not getting anything done, Tommy. How long do you think this flying thing will last? It's going to become something like the hula hoop. Yeah, sure it's fun for a while, but eventually people are going to get bored with it and realize there are some important things that need to be done. Who's going to do those important things, Tommy? People who are flying in the air like a bunch of bird brains? I'll tell you who is going to be doing it—Bill McCall and people who believe in hard work and a fair day's pay.

DOC BIRD: You're again talking about something you know nothing about, Bill. Why don't you tell us about Vietnam? Oh, right, you've never been there. Then why not tell us about flying? Oh, right, you've never done that. That's the hard work you're talking about, Bill, the hard work of lying and talking about things you have no first-hand knowledge of—

73

Hypocrisy is something we experience throughout our lives. Someone tells us something that they are guilty of and tries to criticize us citing shortcomings they possess. It happens all the time. Someone who repeats things all the time will criticize someone for repeating himself. Someone who is loud and abrasive will point out how loud someone else is. Yes, it happens all the time.

Yes, Doctor Nutt, do you think it is happening now more than ever?

I think people hear politicians and try to emulate them. There are some politicians who say they value the human life and then support sending troops to foreign lands to fight a war. There are others who say they value the human life and therefore oppose abortions, but proclaim their support for the death penalty. It happens all the time. I hear people accusing each other of being obnoxious and crude. You hear them swearing at each other and wonder who the obnoxious and crude ones are and who are the ones being unfairly criticized. Yes, there's a lot of hypocrisy out there.

This has been going on for a long time, hasn't it?

Oh, yes, definitely. Jesus talked about hypocrisy when he found the elders counting money in their place of worship. He attacked them for mixing materialism with spirituality and tried to explain how spirituality was the more valuable of the two. Yes, there's been hypocrisy throughout human history. People accusing other people of the very same thing they were guilty of. The fat man laughs at someone for eating too much, the skinny man laughs at the person who doesn't eat.

Yes, that's very interesting, Doctor Nutt. Who do you end up believing?

Everyone tell their own tales. Only God would be able to decipher who was telling the truth and who was lying. But when one person says one thing and then does another, or criticizes someone for doing something that they themselves have done, well, then, you have to say this was another example of hypocrisy. We see hypocrisy at its worst in politics and the world around us. A politician who rails against eroding social values and then is caught cheating on his wife with another woman is one example. Politicians screaming drill, baby, drill, and then accusing their opponents of wrongdoing when there is a catastrophic oil spill is another. I'm sure you can think of many examples yourselves. It happens all the time in our society. Someone is criticized for incompetent behavior on the job and then the person doing the criticizing makes a monumental mistake.

Yes, we're talking to Doctor Albert Nutt. We'll be back after these very important messages—

Bill McCall says he's served in Vietnam. But that was a lie. He's said he has balanced the budget, but that was a lie. Now he says flying without any mechanical assistance has no real point to it. But how would Bill McCall know? He's never tried it. Tired of politicians saying and doing the same old thing? Vote for Doctor Tommy Hagenhurst. Doc Bird will do all the things Bill McCall just talks about. He will balance the budget and teach people how to fly. All Bill McCall can do is talk and lie. Vote for Doctor Tommy Hagenhurst.

I'm Doc Bird and I wholeheartedly approve this message—

Flying will bring about the next technological era in American history. First, there was the horse and then the railroad. An interstate highway system opened the country to automobiles and now there's a new way that will be more time-saving and convenient. This then will be the new technological and medical revolution: flight without mechanical assistance.

Yes, Dr. Jabber, that's very interesting. Will it change everything?

Things that don't change eventually erode. It's the same with societies and art forms. Those that don't change eventually erode away and fall into decadence. Flight without mechanical assistance is the change that will revitalize our society. It will bring about a civil rights revolution as well. There will soon be no reason to be prejudiced. Everyone will be flying off to new locations in a fraction of the time it used to take. And everyone will have access to places once thought of as hard to get to. Not with Doctor Tommy Hagenhurst's flying serum. Now everyone will be able to fly to any place they choose and they will get there sooner than ever. It really is the next revolution in American family life.

So then you think everyone will fly?

Eventually, yes. You see the status quo will take its time evaluating this new revolution and decide whether it will participate. Those that reject the status quo will be flying very soon. As I've said before, new societies and art forms must adopt and adapt new technologies or face decadence and eventual destruction. That's why painting evolved through the years. No one wants to do the same thing over and over again forever. So first there was a rejection of the human form and abstraction became popular. Abstraction led to found art and performance art and so on. If painting had stayed with the human form, it eventually would have become decadent and no longer a reflection of the society that produced it. Those are some of the reasons to reject the status quo and progress into the future.

But the status quo still rules the society, is that not true?

Yes, but eventually the status quo even understands the importance of change and progress. Many fields become stagnant after a while because the status quo develops rules and regulations that keep people out of the field they wish to participate in. It happens all the time. Look at publishing, books began to look and read the same, and the publishing field developed rules and regulations that kept new writers with bold, new ideas out of the system. But technology knows nothing about these rules and regulations and tends to open things up for everyone. For example, the publishing industry will be changed by the internet and computers whether it likes it or not. Many rules and regulations will fade until new writers will have access to the open marketplace. People who would have no access because they lacked an agent or a huge publisher, would now have an opportunity to have people read their material without any middle man.

Yes, how else will flying change the society?

Well, as I said, there will be a civil rights revolution as well. No longer will there be any distinction between black and white or any other ethnic group. In the future, everyone will be able to fly and everyone will be able to free themselves from the status quo. In the past, the status quo produced an unfair society, but with new technology and medical advances, things will become more equal. Everyone will be able to fly and everyone will take advantage of the benefits. It will be another Civil War in which the members of the society will be fighting for the rights of all its citizens. That's the value of flying without mechanical assistance.

Will we see those advances right away?

Yes, I believe we will see the advances almost immediately. As soon as people take to the air, the society will begin to change for the better. It will be a new revolution in travel and living. It will advance society like interstate highways advanced the society in the 1950s. It will advance society like the transcontinental railroad advanced society in the 1800s. It will advance society as much as the wheel did all those centuries ago. Yes, and with advancement will come great changes for the society and when the society changes, so does its art and values. For example, the human form was rejected in art with the development of photography. Television and movies made the society a more visual one. Yes, and now with flying and computers, the society will gain and use information more rapidly than in the past. Society will once again change to one based on speed and video information.

Thank you, Dr. Jabber, we'll be right back—

74

I wasn't feeling too well. All the years of making love to so many men and women began to have an effect on me. I still had something like AIDS and now it was beginning to destroy my health. The doctors said I didn't have long to live. I decided I would do everything I could to last until the election. There was no way I was quitting in the middle of something that was so important. Whether I was sick or not and whether that had affected my brain did not concern me, I was staying in the race until the end.

The real joy I had was being with my family of 187. Yes, 187 members of a family that Letty and I had started from scratch. We truly believed we were helping the world by adopting these children from all over the globe. We cared for these children as if they were our own, and hopefully, gave them a better life than they ever would have had without us.

"You were good to us, doc," Keisha once said to me. "That's why I'll love you no matter what you do."

"Yes, and I'll love all of you no matter what happens to me in the future," I told her. "You see we realize how much of a commitment we made to each other and therefore, will stick with each other no matter what happens."

"Yes, doc, we might not approve of what you have done, but we know you always loved us. We know by your actions and words that you always cared about what happened to us whether you were there or not."

Keisha's words had a big effect on me. I started to rethink my positions on a lot of the issues in the campaign. With love soothing my soul, I decided that maybe I should tell people I was against war and the death penalty. I was in favor of letting a woman decide what was best for her body, although I still felt life began in the womb at conception. There were so many new things I thought about and decided that I should do the right thing before it was my time to go.

I told Letty what I was planning and she gave her support. The children also thought it was a good thing for me to tell the people how I felt. It didn't matter to me that it was very close to the election. I had to do what I thought was right. The people should be voting for the person who best represented the good of society, I told myself, and therefore, I would change my positions to the ones I thought would be best for society.

I really didn't care how the people, the media, or my opponents would react. They would probably call me a "flip-flop" or a hypocrite. I didn't care. All I wanted now was to do the right thing for the people and the society, and the right thing entailed peace and harmony in the world.

"You're doing the right thing, Tommy," Letty assured me. "Once the people hear how you've changed, you'll win the election without any problem."

"Yes, and I still plan to teach all of them to fly," I replied.

"That's just a bonus," she said to me. "What the people want to hear is that they'll be safe and secure in the new world we have planned."

Letty was so right. I would assure the people that if they voted for me they would be safe and at peace in a world in which they would all learn to fly. I only hoped I had the time to carry out my plans.

75

Let Doctor Tommy Hagenhurst lead us into the new world. A new world of peace and contentment. No wars. No death penalty. Nothing to disturb our utter happiness. That's the kind of world Doctor Tommy Hagenhurst wants. He'll help teach everyone how to fly without mechanical assistance. He'll help all of us live in peace and harmony. Let's follow Doc Bird to the new world. Vote for Doctor Tommy Hagenhurst for the U.S. Senate. You and your loved ones will be glad you did.

I'm Doc Bird and I enthusiastically approve this message—
Doctor Tommy Hagenhurst for Senate.

BILL McCALL: Oh, now he wants us all to live in peace and fly around the planet like white doves. What's next, doc? I mean can anyone believe anything this man says? First, he has affairs with men and women and then he says he loves his wife and 187 adopted and natural children. Then he says he wants a good war. Now he says he wants peace and love for everyone. Can anyone keep track of his positions? He jumps around more than a Mexican jumping bean.

DOC BIRD: Bill McCall is *muy loco*. He's the one who keeps changing his mind about his past. First, he's a veteran in the Vietnam War. Then he was nowhere near Vietnam, shuffling papers in the United States. Then he says he has experience balancing a budget, but no balanced budget was ever produced. Can anyone keep track of Bill McCall?

BILL McCALL: What are you talking about, Doc Birdbrain?

DOC BIRD: Bill McCan't!

BILL McCALL: Go off flying into the wild blue yonder, you dodo. You want the people to follow you into the new world? Where is it, doc? In some cuckoo's nest? Now if you want to have a good life without soaring off to

God knows where, then you'd better vote for me. Following this birdbrain will lead you to a whole lot of trouble.

DOC BIRD: The only birdbrain is someone who doesn't want to take advantage of the new way of life. My serum will revolutionize American family life. No longer will we be dependent on such out of touch gasbags like Bill McCall. The planet will be ours to do with as we want. There will be freedom and liberty just as we were promised. You want to follow Bill McCall back to the Dark Ages or do you want to follow me to a new world of peace and flight? Don't get left behind, people.

BILL McCALL: The only place Doc Birdbrain will take you is where the dodo went. Don't be fooled, people. This so-called scientist is nothing but another nutty professor. He wants to lead you to a place where everybody is flying around doing nothing. We are not comic book characters who don't want to do anything but fly around. We want to learn, live and be happy. This is what you'll get from Bill McCall.

DOC BIRD: Flying is not some scheme to waste time, Bill. It's a veritable revolution in travel and family life. You make it sound as if it's some child's toy to fool around with. It's more like an adult plan to change the world. This is something you once again failed to grasp as it pertains to the real ramifications. You failed to grasp the consequences of not having a balanced budget, and now you fail to grasp the ramifications of something that will revolutionize this country. You're not qualified to be a U.S. Senator, Bill. Grasp that fact and admit it. Grasp something.

BILL McCALL: I would grasp you, but you would probably like that, Tommy. Like all those men you slept with. Disgusting. And what about all those women you slept with. Disgusting. Now you want all of us making love on the top of Mount McKinley. Men and women and who knows what. What kind of ethics and morals do you have, Tommy?

DOC BIRD: I have enough ethics and morals to understand, Bill. When I was saving all those people, no one questioned my ethics and morals. I got the job done. And I'll get the job done again if you elect me your next senator. I understand people, Bill, unlike you. I understand their needs and wants and I want to do what's best for them. That's what I've always done. You don't understand anything, Bill. You haven't done a darned thing for the people in all your years in politics. I don't think you ever plan on doing anything for the people. All you care about are status and materialism.

BILL McCALL: And all you care about is shooting your gun off in everybody's business. Go fly off to fag land, you cuckoo bird.

That concludes our last debate between Doctor Tommy Hagenhurst and Bill McCall, candidates for the U.S. Senate—

76

Our top story tonight is Doctor Tommy Hagenhurst's victory in today's primary. Hagenhurst, who promised the voters he would teach all of them to fly without mechanical assistance and then changed his positions on the issues, won by a comfortable margin over his opponent, Bill McCall. The final totals had Doctor Hagenhurst with 62 percent of the vote and McCall with 30 percent. The other candidates in the race divided up the remaining votes. For Hagenhurst, this is his first political win. He now goes on to face Carl Hayes in the general election. Barry Juggins is standing in Hagenhurst campaign headquarters and has this report—

Doctor Hagenhurst, also known as Doc Bird, was ecstatic tonight as he claimed victory in the primary against Bill McCall. He said he was confident he would defeat Carl Hayes in the upcoming general election and become the state's next United States senator.

"No one will stop us in our quest for freedom and independence. Not Bill McCall and not Carl Hayes. The people of this state want something better for the future and I will help them attain everything they're after."

Doctor Hagenhurst speaking to his supporters after the final vote was announced. His wife, Letty or JetLet, was at his side as he made his victory announcement, although only a handful of his estimated 190 children were at the podium. When asked if everybody will be flying after the general election, Doctor Hagenhurst said this:

"Yes, we'll all be flying to new places, seeing new faces, and participating in the revolution that will be ours for the asking. Everyone will be welcomed, friend and foe alike, and together we will build a great nation, a nation of freedom and cooperation."

It is not known how many people have already learned to fly from Doctor Hagenhurst on the campaign trail, but it is a significant number. Whether he keeps his promise to teach the rest of the population how to fly without mechanical assistance will be seen in the weeks ahead. Right now, supporters say, the doctor has to concentrate on defeating Carl Hayes. Only after that is achieved, they say, will he begin teaching everyone how to soar into the clear, blue skies.

Reporting from Hagenhurst campaign headquarters, this is Barry Juggins—

Tell us now, Doc Bird.

That's what Carl Hayes is asking. He says it's not fair that Doc Bird is using his secret of flight to get elected senator of this state. He says the doc should step forward now and tell us all how to fly. It's a secret that belongs to the people, isn't it? It's a secret that belongs to all of us. Tell us now, Doc Bird. Tell us before the secret is used as a bribe to get elected. Tell us before the voters of this state decide who is more capable of leading this state in the U.S. Senate. Tell us now, Doc Bird.

I'm Carl Hayes, and I approve this message—
Carl Hayes for Senate.

Doctor Tommy Hagenhurst wants everybody to have an equal chance at showing what they can do. He wants to teach everybody how to fly and enjoy their freedom and independence. But there are some hard issues to debate and Doc Hagenhurst wants everyone to understand what needs to be done in the days and years ahead. He has many ideas on what should be done. His opponent can only sit back and attack. Is that what you want from your next senator? Vote Doc Hagenhurst. He'll lead us all into a new world. "Peace is half a fist."

Doc Hagenhurst for U.S. Senate.
I'm Doc Hagenhurst and I wholeheartedly approve this message—

While Doc Bird is flying around, Carl Hayes is asking the questions that need to be asked. How are we going to balance the budget? Do we need to keep the peace in the world? Are our citizens safe? These are the tough questions that need to be answered by someone who is qualified to answer them. We don't need some flying space cadet to lead us into a new world.

The world we live in is fine. It just needs a good leader. Vote for Carl Hayes for Senate. The leader this state needs.

I'm Carl Hayes and I approve this message—

Doc Hagenhurst doesn't need to ask questions. He has the answers. He has the answers to a balanced budget, peace in the world, fighting crime, and showing people how to live a free and happy life. He doesn't need to ask questions. He's already found a solution for making people more free. Yes, this state and country needs a leader. A good leader, a leader who will teach us how to fly into a new age of independence. That's Doc Hagenhurst, a leader who knows what he's doing and doesn't need to ask how to do it. Vote Doc Hagenhurst for U.S. Senate.

I'm Doc Hagenhurst and I enthusiastically approve this message—

Vote Doc Hagenhurst.

Yeah, Gibby, I just got back from flying to Mount Everest. It was way cool and pretty freaky. That scientist dude is unbelievable, man. He injected me with that flying juice and I was up, up and away in no time. Man, it was awesome. You can go anywhere you want, Gibby. I mean coming back from Everest, I watched some of the ball game from over the stadium. It was awesome, man, really awesome. Well, I gotta go, Gibby, I'll be speaking to you in a few, man—

Click to watch video—

Are you going to come flying with me? We're off to new places and new adventures. All you've got to do is trust me.

Look at all the people flying in the skies!

(Video footage of people flying)

Come and join us!

Vote for Doctor Hagenhurst for United States Senate. Join the revolution. Vote Hagenhurst.

END OF VIDEO

77

CARL HAYES: You're a flying fool, doc, but we don't need a flying fool to lead this state, we need someone who is serious and competent.

DOC BIRD: Well, you're certainly not serious and competent, Carl. What the heck have you ever done to better the people of this state? At least, I know something about how government works. I also am prepared to lead this state and the nation into a new era of progress. Flying fool, Carl? Oh, I thought you were more mature than that. We'll all be flying, but we won't be fools. We'll bring about the greatest revolution this country has seen in centuries.

CARL HAYES: Because you can fly doesn't mean you should be a United States senator, doc. I mean if that's the case then I'm voting for a yellow-bellied sapsucker as my next senator. You've got to have more than some crazy promise to lead the people of this state.

DOC BIRD: Crazy promise, Carl? People are already experiencing the freedom of flight while we stand here and debate it. I have already shown the people that this is much more than some crazy promise. It's real, it's reality, and it's already here.

CARL HAYES: Then why are you taunting the people of this state, doc? You'll only teach everybody how to fly if they elect you senator, is that it? That is illegal or something. You can't just hold this flying thing over everybody's head. It's not right, it's not ethical, it's not moral, doc. Can't you understand that?

DOC BIRD: I'm not holding anything over anybody's head. I've already taught a number of people to fly to show that I will fulfill my promise. But there are things that have to be done first before I can concentrate on getting everybody to fly. The people have to decide who is going to lead them in the months and years ahead. That's all that's going on, Carl. Maybe you should look at the news once in a while.

CARL HAYES: I look at the news, you damned cuckoo bird. I see there's an election between one intelligent dude and one who wants to fly away like a little birdie. Well, which should we choose? I know which one I would choose, the intelligent one.

DOC BIRD: We can debate that, too, Carl. I think the intelligent one is Doctor Tommy Hagenhurst, who wants to lead the people into a new age of flight and independence. That would be the wise choice, Carl. The other candidate, Carl Hayes, knows nothing about governing the people. He knows only how to attack the intelligent candidate.

CARL HAYES: Doc, you're the one who knows nothing about governing the people. You've never held an elective office of any kind. How would you know what the people want? You're just trying to trick them into voting for you with talk of flying around like cuckoo birds. I'm the one they should vote for if they want any work to be done. I mean what kind of work are you going to be doing, doc? You're going to be flying around in circles while the people and this state wait for the buzzards to come.

DOC BIRD: I'm not going to be flying around in circles, Carl. That's something you would do. I'm going to be looking out for people and helping them until they know how to help themselves. That's what I'm going to be doing. What will you be doing, Carl? Attacking me while you chase your tail around in circles?

CARL HAYES: I'll chase you right off this stage, doc. You're the one changing his views all the time, ain't that right? I mean you're for war and then peace. Half a fist or not, right, doc? Then you're for less government, a right-winger. Then you say you're for the people and that everyone is welcomed. Which is it, doc? You for the people or the rich? You for killing or keeping peace in the world? Everybody would really like to know what you stand for, doc.

DOC BIRD: I stand for the people and have always stood for the people. No one was questioning my dedication when I was saving people, no one was questioning my dedication when I put my life on the line. I have always been very clear about where I stand. My opponent, meanwhile, is standing in poop. Poop he continually stoops down to pick up and tries to throw at others. What a stinking mess that I'll have to clean up.

CARL HAYES: The only mess is going to be you, doc. I'm going to mess you up pretty good with the truth. Why don't you tell the truth, doc? Why do you tell us one thing and then do another. You're just like all the other politicians, doc. Saying one thing and doing another. Well, Carl Hayes tells it like it is. Always have and always will.

DOC BIRD: You going to tell us how you screwed up again, Carl? That would be the truth. You've been saying nothing, Carl. What I say I mean and have done in reality. What have you done in reality, Carl? I say one thing and the people listen, Carl. What the heck are you talking about? Is anybody listening to you, Carl?

CARL HAYES: I'll tell you who's listening, Tommy, everyone who knows you're full of it. You're just waiting to tell everyone how to fly until you're elected, Tommy, and everyone knows it. You're not qualified to be a senator, but people want to fly. They want to fly so bad they'll elect some novice who knows nothing about being a senator. That's the only way you'll get your votes, Tommy, by bribery. Another unethical politician who wants to run the government, that's who you are, Tommy—

78

The best thing about the election has been the reaffirmation of my love for Letty. I think I understand now how much Letty has meant to me. She has been by my side through so many ordeals that it wouldn't be right if I should ever lose her again. She has been my lover, my wife and mother to my children. She has also been my friend and partner.

"Life is short, but there are things we leave behind," she was saying to me. "Memories are the main thing."

"Will you remember me, Letty?" I asked.

"How could I forget you, Tommy?"

"What will you remember about me?"

"Your face, your eyes, the way you looked flying through the air."

"Is there anything I said that you will remember?"

"What do you mean, Tommy?"

"I mean something to remember me by. Something I said or did which makes me stand out from the rest."

"Well, you did teach everyone how to fly, Tommy. That's something, isn't it? I mean I'll always remember how you told me you loved me. Isn't that something, Tommy?"

"Yes, but how about something I said about the human race."

"Did you say anything about the human race, Tommy?"

"Oh, well, maybe not."

But now I knew, wherever I was going, I was going with Letty. She knew me better than anyone and I knew her better than anyone. We would be together through eternity or something.

"What are you going to do when I become senator, Letty?"

"I'm going to get my hair done and then wait for you to buy me the biggest diamond I've ever seen."

"Is that what you really want, Let?"

"No, Tommy, all I ever really wanted was to be a big and happy family."

"Well, we are now, aren't we?"

'Seems so, Tommy, if you can keep your nose out of trouble."

"I'll be good, Letty."

"I know you will, Tommy, I know you will."

I think Letty knew all the time that my condition was worsening, but she never said anything about it. She knew I was dying and I knew I was dying, but neither of us would really acknowledge it. We just sat there with each other in our arms and talked about the future. We had been through a lot together. The only thing left to say would be good-bye.

79

DOC BIRD: You're not the best man for the job, Carl. You don't know the first thing about government. You've never really accomplished anything in all your years of service. Why don't you just give up now and admit to the people that you're a fraud and not qualified for the job?

CARL HAYES: I'll do it when you admit to the people that the only reason you get one vote is because you promised to make everyone fly. That's all the people want, Tommy, your darned flying juice. They don't care about anything else in this race. Why don't you admit to that?

DOC BIRD: They want more than just flying, Carl. The people are interested in the issues, but they've seen politicians like you before. You go along attacking your opponent and saying nothing new. The people know about you, Carl. It just seems to you that all they want is to fly. They want more. But only I can give it to them, Carl.

CARL HAYES: There's only one thing you can give to them, Tommy, and that's your crazy flying juice. I'll even have to sample it some time. I'll just give up and fly around and around. Nothing better to do, right, Tommy? Oh, the people want more, I know that. That's why on Election Day they're going to decide they don't need your stupid flying juice and elect the person who is most fit for the job. That's me, Tommy, me. I'm the most fit for the job of United States senator. And you, Tommy, are most fit for the cuckoo nest.

DOC BIRD: You're not fit for anything, Carl. You can call me cuckoo, but we'll see who the crazy one really is. You're the one who can't accept reality. There are plenty of people already flying around out there and you still can't accept it. I'd say there's actually something wrong with you, Carl. My flying juice is going to change the entire world, Carl, and then maybe you'll see how wrong you are about flying and everything else.

CARL HAYES: Don't believe him, ladies and gentlemen. He's never going to share the secret of unaided flying. The joke's on all of us. That's the kind of person Tommy is. When that's all we care about, Tommy's going to disappoint us all in the end. He's never going to tell us the secret of flying. Isn't that right, Tommy?

DOC BIRD: Carl doesn't know what he's talking about. He never did know what he was talking about. I'm going to share the secret with everyone very soon. That day is surely going to come, but right now I must convince the voters that I am the best person to be senator. Don't listen to Carl, he had never known the truth about anything. The voters know and that I'm confident about.

CARL HAYES: All the voters know, Tommy, is that you're going to teach them to fly. Well, are you going to teach them, Tommy? Or is that another campaign promise you have no intention of keeping? We want to fly now, Tommy, why do we have to wait? You're holding the voters hostage, Tommy, until you're elected a senator of this great state. Well, I say that stinks. Yes, stinks and should be illegal. Holding everyone a hostage until you figure out whether you want to tell us or not.

DOC BIRD: I'll tell everyone, Carl, and then what will you say? That you're more qualified to be elected senator? What a laugh. This is someone you could never trust with anything let alone the government of this great state—

80

Will we ever learn the secret of unaided flight? That's the question tonight as Senate candidate Carl Hayes charged that Doctor Tommy Hagenhurst does not intend to ever reveal the hush-hush secret. We take you to the site of tonight's debate where Lisa Barlow is standing by. Lisa?

Yes, I'm here at the debate site where Carl Hayes repeatedly attacked Doctor Tommy Hagenhurst for not revealing the much awaited secret of unaided flight. At one point, Hayes charged that Hagenhurst, also known as Doc Bird, never intends to ever tell the people the highly guarded secret.

"He's just playing with us," said Hayes. "He's never going to tell us the secret because he knows once the secret is revealed, he's totally useless."

Hagenhurst laughed at the charges and told this reporter, "The secret will be revealed very shortly. No one, however, is going to force me to reveal it before I intend."

There are some people who already have sampled Hagenhurst's flying concoction and have proven it works. Many of them report being able to fly to distant places just as Doctor Hagenhurst promised. The people, however, still have to decide whether they will vote for Hagenhurst for United States senator. His opponent, Carl Hayes, says just because Hagenhurst can fly doesn't mean he's qualified to serve in the Senate.

"He's just some crazy scientist," Hayes said. "He's not qualified to be a U.S. senator, everybody knows that."

Well, some people might disagree. According to the latest polls, Hagenhurst leads Hayes by at least ten percentage points with the election only a week away.

"We'll be making up the deficit in the coming days," said one Hayes pollster. "His words have had a great effect on the voting public."

The Hayes camp also thinks they will get some help in the polls with Hayes' victory in tonight's debate. At least that's the way they see it.

"Hayes definitely exposed Hagenhurst as the lying nutty professor he is," said one Hayes associate. "I think Hayes won the debate and by a large margin. That's going to really help in the last week of the election."

Meanwhile, Hagenhurst's people think that he easily won tonight's debate. "Tommy kept showing how Hayes doesn't really know what he's doing," said one Hagenhurst strategist. "All Hayes kept doing was challenging Tommy to produce the secret to flying. This Tommy will do at the right time and the people understand that."

There's still no word on what the secret to unaided flight is. Doctor Hagenhurst promises he will reveal the secret right after the election this week. No one can force the doctor to produce his so-called flying juice and everyone seems to know that. Many people, however, say they think Hagenhurst will ultimately reveal the secret if he is elected.

Reporting from tonight's debate site, this is Lisa Barlow—

How ill is Doctor Tommy Hagenhurst and will he live for an entire Senate term? We're here with his wife, Letty, to ask the tough questions—

INTERVIEWER: We hear Doc Bird is very sick. Is that true?

LETTY: Tommy has been feeling much better in the last few months and I'm confident he'll be ready to serve in the Senate if he's elected.

INTERVIEWER: Exactly what does Doc Bird suffer from?

LETTY: It's really not that complicated. It's just a combination of exhaustion and hard work. He's really a very dedicated person and it seems he's been trying to do too much.

INTERVIEWER: So then does that mean he'll be all right in the weeks ahead?

LETTY: Yes, I think doc will be fine as soon as he can relax. That probably won't happen until the election is over. Right now, he's just exhausted.

INTERVIEWER: Does he have his own personal physician?

LETTY: Yes, of course. Doc is seeing all of the right people and will definitely be on the road to recovery as soon as he can relax. Right now, he's running on every last ounce of strength he has.

INTERVIEWER: What is your opinion of the election at this point?

LETTY: I think Tommy is doing an excellent job, but the people will ultimately decide. All the polls say Tommy is out in front, but you never know what's going to happen until the votes are cast. I have been very proud of Tommy during this election and hope he succeeds.

INTERVIEWER: Do you think he'll win?

LETTY: I hope so because I love Tommy very much. My whole family loves Tommy and has supported him throughout this campaign. We all hope Tommy wins the election and becomes a senator. It's something he really wants to do.

Thank you Letty Hagenhurst for your time and good luck to Doc Bird in the upcoming election—

Doctor Tommy Hagenhurst, also known as Doc Bird and the fantastic Flying Man, became this state's next United States Senator tonight as we project him the winner in his race with Carl Hayes. With 94 percent of the vote in, Hagenhurst has 59 percent of the vote while Hayes has 36 percent. The new senator has said that if elected he will reveal the secret of unaided flight to everyone. We're now going to go to Hayes campaign headquarters where the candidate will concede defeat—

"We put up a good fight. But my opponent had something everyone wanted and that was that secret of flight. Hopefully, let it be everything the people hoped for. I just pray to God that nothing bad comes of learning Tommy's big secret. I want to thank my family and everyone associated with this campaign for their support and hope to see you all again in the future. I want to wish my opponent good luck and thank you all once again."

(Applause)

That was Carl Hayes conceding defeat and now we take you to Hagenhurst headquarters where Doc Bird is going to claim victory in tonight's election—

"Thank you all very much. It was a hard fight, but I had a lot of support in obtaining this great victory. (Applause) Thanks to my wife, Letty, and to my children whose names I cannot recite for fear of taking us too late into the evening. Thanks to my campaign staff and to those who helped get me elected. But most of all, thanks to the people of this great state. (Applause) They are the ones responsible for this fantastic victory tonight. In the days ahead, there will be some great changes and everyone will be involved. We will all be flying off to new places. (Applause) Yes, and we will be discovering things we never knew existed in this great world of ours. (Applause) Everyone will be included and that is my pledge to you on this momentous night. (Applause) I will be honored to be your senator and I know we will do some great things together. The world will never be the same. (Applause) Thank you all very much. Let's get started. (Applause)

Doctor Tommy Hagenhurst making his victory speech tonight as he is the projected winner in the Senate race with Carl Hayes. Doctor Hagenhurst did not specifically say in his speech that he will be revealing the secret of unaided flight, but he seemed to hint that he will tell everyone how it's done in the days ahead—

81

I decided I wasn't going to keep my promise. There was no way I could reveal to the world how unaided flight was accomplished. I had already seen that showing only a few people how to fly caused chaos and reckless behavior. I didn't want to hurt the world, I wanted to help it. By telling everyone how to fly, what would happen to all the lives involved? Would there be utter chaos and confusion? I feared so. I knew the media would hound me for the secret and I knew I had promised the people, but I decided it was better if they didn't know.

The media had made me a rich and powerful man. I was now a United States Senator and I could still fly. But all that would not save me from dying. I knew I didn't have much time left. The disease had spread throughout my body and now I had to decide what I would do about it. There was really only one answer. I would not serve as a U.S. Senator and I knew it. I had known it for a long time, but human beings are selfish and will do anything they can to attain any goals they set for themselves. We are something like cockroaches. No matter what you do to us, we keep on going, spreading our disease of egotism and selfishness throughout the world. I was no different and I knew that. I had been a product of the media and I would not attack it like many other celebrities.

Many celebrities blamed the media for all kinds of problems, when in fact, the media was the only reason these celebrities were known and worshipped throughout the world. They all had publicists and public relations people putting out their names whenever they could. These celebrities became famous and then they attacked the very same people and companies that they had distributed their names to. I vowed I would not do the same.

But this was definitely the end. I had done all I could to become a star in this society. I had been a flying hero, a TV star, a star of commercials, the head of a large and talented family, and now a United States Senator. It had been a good life, but I wondered if anybody would really remember me in a few years. Oh, well, maybe my wife and children would remember, but would that be it? I asked myself why did I need to be remembered and I answered I do not know. It just seems like the thing to do. As a little child, I marveled at people like Shakespeare and Mark Twain being handed down through the ages, and somehow, I wanted the same to happen to me. But did it really matter?

I mean if you look at the best of them, Shakespeare, Michelangelo, Leonardo, Einstein, Newton and the rest, there is really only a very small amount that is remembered. For the rest of us, and that includes most of the celebrities we know or have known, what did they really leave behind? Do you remember anything these famous people said or did? We can remember, "To be or not to be," but what does it really mean? We remember e equals mc squared and know that was part of Einstein's genius, but what does it really mean in the scheme of things? That a mass going the speed of light will produce energy? Well, how does that really help or hurt us in living our lives? And it also brings up the question that if that is not significant, just what is? Is anything we say or do significant at all? What is the real worth of celebrities and celebrity status? Do we really remember anything or anyone in the end? When a celebrity dies, ask yourself if you remember anything they said or did. The chances are they didn't even write the lines themselves!

So now I was a celebrity ready to fly off into the wild blue yonder. Was there anything I said or did that meant anything to anybody? Probably not. I thought about it and decided most lives are insignificant. Probably 99.9 percent. Just what are we peddling, anyway? Most of it is just pure junk. Most of it is senseless and forgettable. Most of us were senseless and forgettable. Newton invented calculus and an apple hit him on the head. Is that meaningful at all? Should Newton be content that he is one of the few that will be remembered? He will be remembered, but for how long? How long will human beings be remembered if the world ended tomorrow? I wondered as I decided what I would do to avoid pain and anguish in the weeks ahead.

I decided I wouldn't serve as Senator. The disease was becoming too painful and was spreading throughout my body. I had to do something to end the pain. I decided I would fly out the window and keep flying up into the air until I could fly no more. I would fly through the atmosphere and likely die before entering outer space. Yes, I would die just as my little boy had died. Oh, poor, Edison, he really did not know what he was really doing. But I do and I decided I would go the same way my boy went. Just like Icarus and Daedalus up into the heavens and then back down to earth. When my wings melted, I fall back down. Just like my poor Edison.

That is the decision I finally made. I decided I wouldn't tell anyone for fear they would try to stop me or inform the authorities. No, this would be my decision alone. I wouldn't tell Letty or the children anything. I would just do it and let things happen. Before walking to the window and flying into the heavens for the last time, I stopped to write something down on a piece of paper. I placed the paper on the table and taped it to the top.

This is what the paper said: Remember me.

Then I flew out the window and into the unknown. Good-bye everybody!